Mansfield Park
in Space

Mansfield Park
in Space

Sybil Nelson

Prologue

Seven Years Ago

"Come on, let me give it a name," Madrick Dashing said from the copilot's seat.

"I really don't see the need," FontL'Roy Darkeny responded.

"What do you mean you don't see the need? Haven't you read any of the ancient space epics? All of the hero teams have awesome names for their spacecrafts. Millennium Falcon, Serenity, Enterprise … Even ships today have names. Why won't you name yours?"

"First of all, this is not a ship; it is a guster, which is why I don't see the need to give it a name."

"I don't see the need. I don't see the need," Madrick said mockingly. "How many times are you going to say that? Your guster might not be a ship, but it is specially designed for interplanetary travel. It needs a name."

"Why can't we just call it a Galvin class guster?"

Madrick sighed. "It's called a Galvin class because it is made out of galvinzinc metal. That is not a name; it is a description. It does not relay the soul of the craft."

Font turned to his friend, confused. "It is a guster. It does not have a soul."

"Dear Gaion, how does Elloree tolerate you?"

"How is Val?" Font asked, attempting to change the ridiculous subject.

Madrick turned around and took a look at his wife. "She is still out from the sedative."

"Do you think she is going to be able to handle this?"

Madrick nodded. "I think she needs this. Once she sees her sister for the first time in thirteen years, she'll be able to close that chapter of her life." He sighed. "And no matter what, I'll be there with her for the next chapter."

"Entering the Necropolis airspace in ten seconds,"

Font said as he began landing procedures.

Ten seconds later, a hologram from the Necropolis Planet Authority appeared on their holophone. "This is the NPA. Please give us your spacecraft name."

Madrick looked at Font. "Told you that you needed a name."

They let Val sleep as they filled out the required documentation and waited for an update. Given that Necropolis was where all the unidentified, unclaimed, and unwanted dead bodies in the galaxy ended up, it would take a while for the sample DNA they provided to be matched.

Both Madrick and Font sat in silence as they waited. Both absorbing the events of the past two weeks. It all started when Font and Elloree had met them on AiJalon with what they thought was good news. Val's sister Dahlonega had been found alive. But when they followed the lead to Kemek, it was anything but good news. What they thought was recent footage of Dahlonega was actually over a decade old and there was no indication that there were any more recent images. The trail had gone cold again.

While on Kemek, however, they were able to find a former henchman of Leaven CoZark and confirmed that he was the one who originally abducted Dahlonega. They also learned that if any of CoZark's girls gave him trouble, he would use his connections to remove their DNA from intergalactic records and then abandon their bodies on Necropolis, which led them to the burial planet this day.

Even though Dahlonega's DNA might not show up on a traditional search, Necropolis was well-known for keeping meticulous internal records. If Dahlonega's body was there, they could find it. Though they all secretly hoped that she wasn't there and still alive somewhere in the galaxy.

Unfortunately, thirty minutes after they arrived, a match was found.

Font and Madrick looked at each other. "Do you want to wake her up or should I?" Font asked.

"I'll do it."

"No need. I'm awake," Val said, standing and heading for the exit of the guster. "Let's get this over with."

They followed a maintenance droid to the Revelation Room where Dahlonega's death pod would be brought for proper identification.

***

Val honestly couldn't tell if they waited two minutes or two hours in that room. She felt as if she were floating both in and out of time. Nothing felt real. Soon, thirteen years of her tireless efforts to find and rescue her sister would come to an end. A fruitless, pointless end.

When the casket entered the room, Madrick and Font stepped back and let Val be the one to inspect the body. The way she immediately collapsed to her knees was the only verification they needed. It really was her sister Dahlonega.

"Madrick, take her back to the guster," Font said. "I'll finish the reclassification of the body."

Given that Val's DNA would easily prove she was the sister, reclassifying the body and having it sent to AiJalon for a proper burial should have been easy. But FontL'Roy Darkeny had learned along the way that anything dealing with Valdosta or Dahlonega Greer was never easy. That turned out to be the case that day as well.

As soon as Madrick and Val left the Revelation room, another maintenance droid entered.

"Did this body have a twin?" it asked Font.

He thought about the years he'd spent with Val searching for her older sister. Never once had she mentioned that Dahlonega was a twin. It wasn't possible.

"Why do you ask?"

The droid checked the records again. "Yes, it is not a mistake. There is another body. It is a genetic match to this one."

Chapter 1

Present Day

About thirty years ago, Miss Me'ordana Ward, a young woman of rather modest finances, had the good fortune to captivate the attention of one Comte Thomas Berzam of Mansfield Park in the Queli archipelago of AiJalon. She thereby was instantly elevated to the rank of Comtesa and bestowed with all the comforts and consequence of a large house and even larger income. It was an unlikely match that was exclaimed as the greatest in Queli history.

Whether the marriage was for money, love, convenience or something else entirely was still unclear even after thirty years.

With Miss Me'ordana Ward so well-attached to a man who owned outright twelve islands in the archipelago, hopes were high for her twin sister Miss Ge'ordana Ward and her older sister Miss Caiana Ward. But there were not so many men of large fortune in the galaxy as there were pretty women who deserved them.

The prospect of marriage for money so frightened Ge'ordana that she determined in her heart quite early in life that she would only marry for love. That love came in the form of a human named Roymund Primme who had no fortune, no education, and no connections to further him in society. Her family felt that she had married merely to disoblige and therefore daily berated her choice, thus forcing her to retreat to the planet Minnith where her husband would still be without fortune, education, and money, but where he would at least be able to find employment and Ge'ordana would be able to live in peace several planets away from her sisters.

Seeing both her younger sisters married before her, one with an advantageous marriage and one with quite an unfortunate attachment, motivated the eldest Miss Ward to accept the proposal of her brother-in-law's elderly friend, the Reverend Emmanuel Norris. Comte Berzam even bestowed upon them a rectory on the premises of Mansfield Park.

Feeling that he had been so generous with one of his wife's sisters, he desired to bestow a gift upon Ge'ordana as well.

His wife, Comtesa Berzam, was a woman of very tranquil feelings who never felt strongly for or against anything and thus had no opinion about such a gift one way or the other. Mrs. Norris, on the other hand, had been endowed with a spirit of activity and what she viewed as justice. And, therefore, she strongly opposed any monetary gift and vowed to devise another gift for her sister that was worthy of the circumstance.

Several years later, the manner in which to bestow a gift upon Ge'ordana had still not been resolved. The strained relationship between the sisters had resulted in little contact over the years, yet Comtesa Berzam and Mrs. Norris were well aware of the dire financial straits their sister was in.

Serves her right, thought Mrs. Norris as she ruminated over each of their marriages. One sister married for money, the other for love; it made sense that *she* would marry for convenience. Though, in truth, Mrs. Norris found nothing convenient about the attachment; although, the lack of poverty was certainly a convenient benefit which she could lord over her younger sister who had married, of all things, a human. A human. What on AiJalon was she thinking? It was an insane decision. And beyond that, she now had a numerous amount of children that she could barely feed. Humans were notorious breeders. Ge'ordana should have realized this and taken the proper precautions. But now she had more children than Mrs. Norris could even count. What was it? Twelve? Thirteen? All she could remember was that it was some outrageous number that began with a T.

If marriage could be compared to the ancient human game of baseball, Me'ordana had hit a home run, Ge'ordana struck out, but Mrs. Norris felt she had at least gotten on base.

"Ten, Mrs. Norris. Ten," Comte Thomas said.

"Sorry, what?" she replied.

"Your sister has ten children," he said. "You insist on increasing the number each time you mention her brood. Ten is quite a large number on its own, so I really do not know why you find the need to exaggerate it."

"Agreed. It is a very large number. An extremely large number. No wonder she can't afford to care for them."

"Yes, yes." Comte Thomas took a seat next to his wife who seemed not very interested in the difficulties of her twin sister. It wasn't because of any malice of heart; she just tended to agree with whatever was uttered last so as not to upset anyone in the room.

"Thus, it only makes sense that those of us in a better position financially should help her in any way we can. Is it not what Gaion would want?"

"Yes, yes," Comte Thomas said again. "What say you, my dear?"

"Oh, well—" Comtesa Berzam began.

"There is no need to bother Comtesa Berzam with this. We don't want to weigh her mind," Mrs. Norris said. "Don't worry at all about this, dear sister. I will take care of everything. That is why I suggest the best way to support our poor, unfortunate sister is to close one of those many mouths."

"Oh my," Comtesa Berzam said, reaching for her medicine which was mostly Engorian wine with barely a whiff of medicinal herbs.

"Do you think ... ? Oh, now I don't mean 'close' the mouth ... I mean ... I mean that we should take one of her children off of her hands. I mean closing the mouth in the sense that we should now feed that mouth instead of her. We can also give her an education and thus more opportunity in life even though she is a human."

"The eldest daughter is now fifteen years of age," Comte Berzam said. "Is it wise for us to take on such a responsibility? How will it affect our own children of similar age?"

"I have put much thought in this and I feel we have nothing to fear," stated Mrs. Norris briskly. "Given her low birth status, we will have no fear of her being in competition for marriage mates with young Marziah and Ju'Lya even though she is close to their ages of fourteen and sixteen. And given that we are family, there is no chance that Thom or Edwin would ever give her a second glance in that way, especially if they are raised as brothers and sister.

Thom is already nineteen years old. I am sure he has already settled in his mind the type of woman he wants. A half-human cousin would be far out of the realm of possibility. And we all know that Edwin ... Well, Edwin is definitely well suited for the life of chastity that he has chosen. So, there is no danger there."

"Your reasoning seems to be correct. And it has been far too long since I made good on my plan to help your sister in some way. We can turn the human child into a respectable woman and set her up gainfully for the future so that she may forever be able to continue helping her family. Also, I am sure she will fill the emptiness of your home since it is just you, Mr. Norris, and the droids."

Mrs. Norris looked taken aback. "Fill *my* home? Why on AiJalon would she be filling *my* home?"

Comte Thomas set down his glass. "Well, since this was your idea and you made all the arrangements, I thought sure you had in mind that she would live with you?"

"I never had such a thought! Why would I think that?"

Comte Berzam said, "We have four children and you have none? It is only logical—"

Mrs. Norris shook her head disapprovingly. "Because you have four children, you are tremendously more equipped to handle one more. I have no children and have never had one. I haven't the slightest idea what to do with one."

"What do you mean? You practically raised your nieces and nephews."

"Yes, yes, but from a distance. I am excellently capable of raising children from a distance. I may be the best there ever was at such. But having a child live with me? Well, that cannot be. My time is completely occupied by taking care of dear, sick, and *old* Mr. Norris. He is in no position to handle the loud interactions of a wild human child. Why, Mr. Norris could no more handle a child than he could fly."

"Then I suppose we should take her," Comtesa Berzam said suddenly. Both Comte Berzam and Mrs. Norris thought she had fallen asleep. Apparently, they were mistaken.

"Then it is settled," said Comte Berzam. "We shall take the child. But solely on a trial basis. If her disposition is really bad, we must, for the sake of our own children, discontinue with the arrangement." Comte Berzam stood and paced the room. "We must prepare the children for the worst so that they may not be too shocked."

Chapter 2

There were a lot of differences between AiJalon and Minnith. It wasn't that Minnith was a poor planet ...Well, it was poor but by choice. Minnithites chose to celebrate the beauty in austerity. They thought glory should go to Gaion and not to themselves so flashy gusters and expensive island gowns were basically unknown there. Instead, most inhabitants of Minnith wore plain frocks so that their beauty came from their countenance and not their outward embellishments.

How the two planets were established was different as well. Minnith was the only planet specifically founded for religious purposes.

It was a place where religions of many different races could gather to worship in peace and thus unite the people of the entire galaxy. Things like war and violence were unheard of on Minnith and it had stayed that way for hundreds of years. It was a planet of refuge where even criminals could flee and so long as they rejected their prior form of life and adopted the teaching of any of the hundreds of religions on the planet, they could live in peace.

Femili Primme had never left her home planet of Minnith before. She had never even left her home sector before and now she would be traveling to a completely different planet with another language, new customs, and a lack of respect for humans. What made her even more anxious, however, was leaving her younger siblings. Part of her didn't even understand why she had to go. Yes, her parents had a lot of children, but Femili was fifteen. She was old enough to help with the raising of the other children. Why send her away?

Her mother, Ge'ordana Primme, gave the excuse that because Femili looked the most AiJalonian, she would fit in the best on AiJalon.

While that was true, she still didn't understand why that mattered. She was still half human. Would she get along better there just because she *looked* AiJalonian? If that was the case, she could definitely do without such a superficial existence. It wasn't something she was used to on her home planet.

Minnith was different from other planets she had heard or read about. Or at least that was what Femili believed with all her heart. On Minnith, things like purity and piety were the most valued and important. Looks and social status were secondary. She had heard stories and read books about how things were on other planets and could scarcely believe the way some people behaved. They married for money and convenience and then just proceeded to have affairs for the duration of their supposed union. It was shameful and sacrilegious.

To her knowledge, the planet Lumerca was the worst offender. Instead of Gaion, those people worshiped money. AiJalon was not much better.

They valued money nearly as much as the Lumercans, but they at least viewed traditions and propriety as important as well. They actually had a Ministry of Purity.

It could never measure up to the elevated standards of purity on Minnith, but at least it was something. Maybe AiJalon wouldn't be so bad.

"When am I to return, Mother?"

Her mother cast her eyes downward and shook her head slowly. "My dear girl, why would you ever want to return here?"

"What do you mean? This is my home. This is where you and Father are! This is where—" She started to name all of her siblings, but honestly she had too many and the ship was due to arrive any moment so instead she just said, "This is where my family is."

"And we will always be here. Trust me. If you ever need to return for any reason, we are here for you. But please don't."

"What?"

"If you love me, please never return to Minnith. You don't belong here."

Femili felt pained. How could her own mother be saying this to her?

"What do you mean?"

"Look at yourself, Femili. You are beautiful. Truly gorgeous. Inside and out. You are wise beyond your years. You are sweet and kind. You are so much more than what Minnith has to offer. Go and find your place in the galaxy."

In truth, Femili had often looked at herself and wondered why she was so different. Why was her hair thicker and more prone to grow out rather than down like most humans? Why was only her skin the color of warm chocolate while that of all of her siblings more resembled caramel? Even her facial features made her stand out from her younger siblings. Femili's nose, mouth and cheekbones were pronounced and striking while all everyone else the family had features that were decidedly flat and unremarkable.

Self-consciously, Femili touched the spiral markings are her neck. Her mother claimed they were simply a scar received after a fall when she was small. But in the back of her mind she always wondered how an accidental fall could result in three perfectly symmetrical spirals.

"Mother," Femili said through tears, "I feel as though you are casting me aside forever."

Ge'ordana Primme hugged her daughter tightly. "I am not casting you aside. I am casting you forward. I am doing the best I can for you. And the best I can do is give you a chance to have a happy future."

"But I *am* happy with you."

"We lead a miserable existence, Femili, and you know it. We barely scrape by. Our success is measured by whether all twelve of us get to eat twice in one day. This is not what you were born for. My only regret is that it has taken me this long to give you a chance to find what you deserve."

Find what I deserve? The words of her mother played over and over again in Femili's mind. What was it exactly that she deserved? Why was it different from what her sisters and brothers deserved?

She just couldn't figure it out no matter how hard she tried. Instead, she tried to shake the thoughts from her mind and focus on her immediate future. She was headed to AiJalon. Shallow, materialistic AiJalon. But while she was there, she would make the best of it. She would work hard and send as many credits as she could back home to support her family.

Her cousins paid for her journey on a transport freight. It was a journey that would take eight hours.

They could have sent her on a faster vessel, but she didn't mind. She would have time to read, pray, and gather her thoughts. Femili felt she needed a mental adjustment in order to view her situation in a more positive light.

Femili traveled on the ArgonLight, a freight vessel designed for transporting goods that could be damaged by vehicles traveling at the speed of light like most modern spaceships. Femili chose to believe the reason her cousins decided to send her on such a slow and antiquated vehicle was because they considered her precious cargo. *Yes, that was it,* she told herself. It definitely was not any kind of foreshadowing as to how she would be treated once she arrived at Mansfield Park.

As she boarded, Femili notice an elderly woman having difficulty with her luggage.

"May I help you, madame?" Femili asked, lifting her bag before awaiting a response.

"Oh, aren't you sweet?" she responded. "How did you know I was a madame?"

Femili smiled. "In preparation for my journey to AiJalon, I have extensively studied their traditions and customs. The color of your monochromatic clothing unit indicates your status, Madame."

"Aren't you a bright girl?" the woman said.

"Thank you, madame. May I ask, where are your servant droids? A lady of your status should not be traveling alone."

The madame sighed. "It seems I bought too many goods on my journey to Minnith. I had to use my servant droids to carry the goods which left me unattended."

"If you will allow it, madame, I can accompany you and be of assistance."

"I would be delighted."

Madame Noonan was the name of the woman who quickly became a best friend and mentor to the young Femili during their eight-hour journey.

"So, you say your mother is from the Queli Archipelago on AiJalon?" Madame Noonan asked as they sipped Gadola tea in her private compartment.

"Yes, madame. She married my father then settled on Minnith where he could find work."

"Find work? On Minnith? Where there are more churches than people? Unless he is a minister, what work could there be there? Why did he not stay on AiJalon?"

Instead of answering immediately, Femili took a sip of tea.

She would have to get used to this line of questioning. On Minnith, the first question was usually "How has Gaion blessed you today?" On AiJalon it was most likely to be "Who are your parents and what do they do?"

Femili took a deep breath. "My father is human. Sot, there is really no place for him on AiJalon outside of a paedor."

Madame Noonan set down her cup of tea and gave Femili a quizzical look. "Are you suggesting that you are half human?"

"I am not suggesting at all, madame. I am stating plainly that my father is indeed human."

Madame Noonan shook her head. "That is not possible. And I am not sure how you have been so misguided."

"I am not sure what you mean," Femili said as she, too, set down her cup. She wasn't sure whether to feel complimented or offended by the madame's words.

"I have been around a long time. I have seen a lot of misturas and none of them have looked like you. Nothing against humans, but you, my dear, are a pure AiJalonian."

Physically, humans and AiJalonians were similar in that they both had two eyes, two ears, and a mouth etc.

But there was much more variability in human genes. Humans had multiple hair colors, for example.

Also, their faces tended to be rounder and duller. One human writer once described the differences by comparing a greyhound dog to a pug. They are both dogs, but by just a glance, one can easily tell which is which.

Another difference was the markings on the neck. All AiJalonians could trace their family lineage back to the twelve founding families of the planet. The purer your blood line, the more prominent your markings. Mixing with certain species, however, would completely prevent the markings from ever developing.

Femili smiled. She worked hard not to make it a condescending smile. But really, this elderly AiJalonian had no idea what she was talking about.

"Madame, if I am pure AiJalonian it would mean one of two things. Either my father is pretending to be human when he is really AiJalonian—which makes zero sense. Why would he choose to be ostracized? If he were going to lie about his genetics, why not choose Engorian or Pentaline?"

"I agree, that is quite illogical," the madam acquiesced.

"—or, I am not my father's child. My mother had an affair with an AiJalonian after giving up her home, status, income and livelihood for the love of a human. For some women, that may be possible, but my mother is a true romantic. If she loved an AiJalonian enough to give herself to him, she would have just married him."

Madame Noonan took a sip of tea to keep herself from spouting out any number of possible scenarios. Namely, what if Femili's mother had had an affair with a married man and then married the human to cover it up? Admittedly, she was not well-acquainted with Femili's mother and thus could not make a judgment call on her character. Instead, she decided to offer proof.

"I have amongst my belongings a monochromatic clothing unit that should fit you. Would you do me the honor of wearing it?"

After Femili changed into the MCU that Madame Noonan provided, the madame said, "Hmm, it is exactly as I suspected."

"What? What is?"

"I shall style your hair before I let you see for yourself."

It took an additional two hours for the madame to style Femili's hair in the way that she saw fit. All the while, the madame shared stories about her life that were so fantastic they sounded like fiction.

Femili couldn't believe the amount of wealth and adventure the madame had enjoyed throughout her life. Surely, the galaxy was indeed wide and Femili wondered if she would ever get to know more of it.

Finally, it was time for Femili to see the revised version of herself. Her image was so striking that even she was beginning to doubt her mother's fidelity. "This is insane," Femili said.

"Indeed, it is. I need something stronger than this tea." Madame Noonan poured a glass of Gadola wine for the two of them.

"I'm only fifteen," Femili said when Madame Noonan offered her the wine.

"Dearie, we are currently in interplanetary space. There are no laws. And I think you will need at least a sip of this in order to process what I am about to tell you."

Reluctantly, Femili took a sip of the wine. It was sweeter than she expected and proved to instantly calm her nerves.

Though she didn't want to admit it, she had become a little nervous at her own reflection. There was honestly not a hint of humanity in her. And with her hair up in the intricate braiding pattern done by the madame, the markings on her neck were rather prominent.

"I am sure you can see what I see," the madame began. "You are without a doubt a pure AiJalonian. And the markings on your neck indicate something more. They indicate that someone has been lying to you for your entire life."

Femili smiled politely and set down her wine after just one sip. Maybe there was some hallucinogen in the drink that had made the madame imagine this elaborate plot. Pure AiJalonian? Markings on her neck?

"Madame, I know what you're thinking. But how could I possibly be part of the royal line when my mother isn't?" Femili began removing the monochromatic clothing unit the madame had given her.

"No, my dear, you may keep it. I surely cannot fit it anymore. And you look far more beautiful than I ever did in it."

Femili was so relieved to have Madame Noonan's company as they departed the ArgonLight. The Cosmo space station was vaster than she could have ever imagined. And there were more people in this station than probably on the entire planet of Minnith. It was a little overwhelming for her.

Looking around she knew there were multiple species populating the space station as Cosmo was a common tourist attraction and travel hub for other destinations, but everyone looked so similar. Due to the monochromatic clothing units, the only differentiation between most beings was the color MCU they had been assigned by their species. If not for Madame Noonan, Femili would have been forced to walk around in a Minnithian frock sticking out like a sick vendula bird. (They changed from a pleasant pink color to a violent red when they were ill.)

***

So, it happened that when Femili exited the spacecraft at the Cosmo station, she was not wearing the customary Minnithian frock for unmarried women that Edwin expected to see. A half-human, half-AiJalonian woman in Minnithian clothing was nowhere to be found anywhere.

Instead, what he saw exiting the ArgonLight was the girl he wanted to marry.

All thoughts of meeting his cousin immediately vacated his mind. Femili who?

He had read about love at first sight in ancient books but didn't think the feeling was possible. That was until he felt it.

The girl he saw looked like she was AiJalonian royalty yet she was helping an elderly woman with her luggage. His heart melted. Her kind eyes and smile convinced him that this was a common occurrence for her. No matter her status, she didn't feel like she was above anyone. She was willing to help anyone in need. How could someone be so beautiful and so kind at the same time? He never even dreamed it was possible.

"May I be of assistance?" he asked, approaching them. But just as he said the words, he tripped and fell down the short flight of stairs that separated them. He landed practically on top of his dream girl. This was not how he wanted the first interaction to go.

Femili dropped the madame's bags and instead reached out to keep him from hitting the ground.

"It seems as though *I* will be assisting *you*," she said with a smile and a giggle as she helped him to his feet.

"I am so sorry," he said. "And so embarrassed."

"Don't be, dear," said the madame.

"Yes, don't be," Femili added. "It wasn't actually your fault. And if you help me with the madame's luggage I will tell you exactly why you fell."

Intrigued and excited, Edwin quickly picked up all the bags and followed them.

Edwin and Femili helped Madame Noonan load her service droids and cargo into her private guster. When they were finished, Madame Noonan grabbed Femili's hand and said, "I wish you all the best. I hope you find your true path. If you ever need any assistance, remember my name and find me."

"So you promised to give me a diagnosis," Edwin said once the madame's guster had piloted away.

"Ah yes." Femili took a cloth handkerchief out of her bag and handed it to him. "Hold this to your ear and tilt your head to the left."

When Edwin did as she suggested, he noticed liquid came out. He repeated the process to the right and, yes, more liquid.

"I suspect you went for a swim this morning. Most likely in a magnetic pond."

She was correct. How did she know?

"I have read that when large cargo ships like the one I was on come into port, the government shifts the magnetic core of the planet
slightly in order to prevent the use of possibly

smuggled equalizers. Because there was water in your ears, it disrupted your body's equilibrium."

Edwin stared at her in amazement. Not only was she beautiful and kind, but she was also intelligent and wise. She couldn't be any more perfect. He had to find out more about her. "Is your family part of the Ministry of Health by any chance?"

She giggled. "No, not by any means. But I do have to go meet my family right now. They are expecting me."

"Can I give you a ride to where you are going? I have my own guster. It's a Galvin class. There are only seven on the planet," he said, hoping she would be impressed.

She smiled and his knees almost buckled. "You're very cute," she said.

"Let us just wait for my cousin to arrive and I will take you anywhere you want to go."

She shook her head. "What would my family think of me if I arrived in a stranger's guster? They might question my judgment and my purity."

"Then have tea with me and we will no longer be strangers."

She paused. Was she contemplating accepting his offer? "You have no idea how attractive your offer sounds," she said finally. "But I really do need to make a good first impression on my family."

In an instant, all sorts of questions about her family situation ran through his head. Given her outfit and her determination to comport herself properly, he finally concluded that she had to be a royal. He didn't want to do anything to put her position in jeopardy.

She turned to walk away, but Edwin grabbed her hand and said, "This may seem very forward of me. I know we just met and you have no idea of who I am or where I come from or if I am trustworthy or not. So I will not pry you for more information about yourself or beg you to take my information so that you may contact me." Slowly and reluctantly, he released her hand, not wanting to frighten her with his advances. "I am not worried about letting you go right now without so much as knowing your name, for I feel that we are meant to be. I am quite confident of it. And if Gaion agrees, I know we will meet again."

Chapter 3

With thirty-eight bedrooms, a ballroom, a conservatory, and several dining rooms, Mansfield Park was essentially a palace and the undisputed grandest home of the Queli Archipelago. Though not the largest home on AiJalon, its unique, classic Roma-Engorian architecture made it stand out amongst other noteworthy homes. Mansfield Park was nestled against a backdrop of lush flora hand selected by Comte Berzam during his intergalactic travels for business. The grounds surrounding the grand home also boasted (not one but two) magnetic ponds, a bioluminescent lake, and several large waterfalls.

Growing up in a home that seemed straight out of a fairy tale book and always having everything they could ever want, had markedly different effects in the Berzam children as evidenced by their reaction to learning about their new permanent resident.

"And where is Edwin?" Comtesa Berzam asked as her other three children gathered before her, her husband, and Mrs. Norris.

"I sent him to meet our guest in Cosmo," Comte Thomas said.

"Guest?" Marziah Berzam asked. "Are we having a guest?"

"More like a permanent resident," Mrs. Norris said.

"What does that mean? Is someone moving in here?" Ju'Lya asked.

"My sister's oldest child will be staying with us," Comtesa Berzam said.

"Your sister ...You mean the one who married a human?" Marziah looked back and forth between her parents in utter shock and confusion.

"Well, that would make her child half human!" Ju'Lya said.

"Excellent job with those calculations, sister. Your studies are really paying off," Thom said.

"Mother, you can't seriously be considering letting a human live here with us," Marziah said.

"Half human. Half," Thom interjected. "I can see you haven't been studying as much as your sister."

"Oh, shut up, Thom!" Marziah searched for something to throw at her brother and decided that a punch would be best.

"Children, stop it!" Comte Berzam said. "Your aunt is very poor and direly needs our help. This is a bit of charity for which Gaion will smile down on us."

"Charity? What are we, an orphanage?" Marziah asked.

"We are not an orphanage. We are family. And family helps one another," Comte Berzam said.

All of the children rolled their eyes simultaneously.

"Now, though she will be living with us, she is not your equal," Mrs. Norris said.

"And is she out as well?" Ju'Lya asked. "I just came out and now I have another girl to compete with?"

"No, no, no. There is no competition. Like you said, she is half human. She probably cannot read. Most definitely cannot speak ancient Ai. I doubt she knows anything of the galaxy. She is likely to be uncultured and barbaric,"

Mrs. Norris said.

"But we mustn't hold that against her. She doesn't know any better and we need to teach her," Comte Berzam said.

"Dear Gaion, will we have to feed her animal flesh?" Ju'Lya asked. "Do they kill the animals with their own hands? Oh Mother, I don't think I can bear it!"

"Children, do not fret," Comtesa Berzam said. "She may be different from us, she may be beneath us, but she is family and we will help her be the best she can be."

"I think they're here!" Ju'Lya yelled, running to the window. It was indeed Edwin's guster that had arrived, but for some reason, only he exited.

"Where is your cousin?" Comte Berzam asked once Edwin entered.

"I looked everywhere, but I did not find a teenage girl wearing a Minnith frock," Edwin said.

"Gaion above! What happened?" Mrs. Norris exclaimed. "Is she lost somewhere in Cosmo?"

"This is a disaster," Comte Thomas said. "She doesn't know anyone. She doesn't know anything about life in the capital. She is completely vulnerable. Someone could easily take advantage of her."

"What if she decided to visit a paedor first? Isn't that where humans crave to go?" Marziah asked.

"What will I tell my sister?" Comtesa Berzam asked. "Ju'Lya, dear, pass me my tonic. This is just too much for my heart."

"Father, I think we should inform the police," Thom suggested. "This could actually turn into a quite serious situation. Human traffickers are on the rise. They do not limit their prey to fully human girls; they actually prefer misturas."

Just when Comte Berzam was about to make the call, they all heard the sound of a tobulon.

Rushing to the window, they stared in awe at what seemed to be a young regal exiting.

What is she doing here? Edwin thought to himself. *Did she find out where I lived so we could continue our conversation?* He silently thanked Gaion above. He knew they were meant to be together. He felt it in every cell of his body.

The servant droid let in the regal and then showed her to the parlor where the family was gathered.

They eyed the young female visitor up and down.

The dark purple monochromatic clothing unit she wore indicated that she was of pure AiJalonian blood, perhaps even of the royal line.

Her dark complexion, sharp features, and gentle smile somehow combined to give her a unique and soft beauty. And the intricate braiding patterns in her hair revealed a level of wealth that rivaled their own. Who was she and why was she there?

Femili felt a bit awkward standing in front of her relations in these foreign clothes. They already didn't know what she looked like, so this clothing unit and hairstyle probably confused them even more. But the amount of staring without talking was going a bit overboard. It had to stop.

"Hello. I am your cousin. Femili Primme." The room gasped collectively.

Comtesa Berzam was delighted that her niece was such a beauty.

Comte Berzam was relieved that his niece would be able to fit in so well. At least they may be able to avoid the outright criticism of having a human living with them.

Mrs. Norris wondered how someone who was half human could look so beautiful. It was wrong and surely a crime against nature. What if someone confused her for a full AiJalonian? Certainly, there had to be a law against her beauty.

Thom was relieved that she was unharmed. His beautiful little cousin would have fetched quite a sum in the underground slave market.

Marziah self-consciously touched her own head regretting not spending a few hours to do her own hair braiding. She leaned for a little and stole a glance of herself in the parlor mirror. She was still prettier, right? Her skin was smooth and dark. Her almond-colored eyes were sharp and elegant. She had been told her greatest feature was her majestic smile. So, she smiled awkwardly making sure she appeared majestic as possible.

Ju'Lya on the other hand focused on her cousin's neck markings. How could they be so prominent when she was only half AiJalonian. Ju'Lya felt her own neck to make sure her markings were still in place and realized her hair was down. Why had she been lazy about her hair today of all days? Ju'Lya was so angry she could scream.

She was sure Marziah was just as livid. But when Ju'Lya looked at her sister, she was...smiling. Should she smile too? Was this some sort of sneak attack? Given that she was virtually a clone of Marziah in looks and personality, Ju'Lya decided to smile as well.

Edwin so devastated he could scarcely breathe. The woman he had fallen in love with nearly at first sight had turned out to be his relation whom he now had to live with and treat as a sister. His world had shattered.

Chapter 4

This was bad. All in the family felt it, except for maybe Comtesa Berzam who had inexplicably slipped into a nap.

Mrs. Norris was the first to state what most in the room were thinking. "This won't do. This won't do at all," she said. "Pray tell us, where did you get those clothes?"

"Oh, a kind AiJalonian woman lent them to me while I was on the cargo transport. She said she wanted to confirm something and then she just let me keep the clothing."

"Well, it is inappropriate for you. How dare a human wear a monochromatic clothing unit reserved for royalty?"

"Half," Thom interjected. "She is half human."

"Whole human, half human. It doesn't matter. She should not be wearing garments for royalty."

"This is for royalty?" Femili asked, looking down at her apparel. "I knew it was for pure AiJalonians, but I had no idea—"

"Did you tell her that you were half human?" Mrs. Norris asked, continuing the verbal assault on Femili.

"Yes, I did. Of course, I did. She didn't believe me."

"Lies. It is not possible. No self-respecting AiJalonian would disgrace her race by allowing a human to wear these clothes."

"Half!" Thom said again. "Half human. And I think she looks quite lovely in them." He gave her a ceremonial bow and then left the room before he became even more irritated.

"Where did this fictitious AiJalonian supposedly get this royal attire?" Marziah could not hide her bitterness even if she wanted to. And since she had no intention of hiding it, all in the room felt it, especially Femili.

"She said she was unable to fit it anymore so I assume it used to be hers," Femili responded, still a bit confused as to why this was a problem.

A shocked silence befell the room once again.

"Are you suggesting you met a member of the royal family?" Comte Thomas asked.

"It would seem so," Femili replied innocently.

"Hoggle swash," Ju'Lya yelled. "If this is true, what was her name?"

"Madame Nocnan."

"See, as I said. Hoggle swash. I have never heard of such a person."

"Well, you wouldn't have," Comte Thomas said. "You are too young. But she is indeed part of the royal family. Or rather, she used to be before a messy divorce nearly thirty years ago."

Mrs. Norris huffed angrily. "Take off those clothes this instant!"

"You mean, right here? Right now?" Femili asked confused.

"No, of course not. Pervert." Mrs. Norris pushed a few buttons on a service droid then said, "Follow the droid."

Femili turned to leave then spotted Edwin. She froze momentarily. What was she supposed to do? The man who had sweetly held her hand and proclaimed that they belonged together was her cousin? It couldn't be.

"Oh, hello," she said to him, trying not to sound too familiar. "Are you my cousin as well?"

Instead of responding, Edwin pressed his eyes closed and turned away.

Femili took that as a 'yes' and continued to follow the droid.

Once she had left the parlor, Mrs. Norris said, "This is serious indeed. More serious than I thought."

"How so?" Comte Thomas asked. "She at least looks the part. Femili should fit in nicely with our family."

Marziah and Ju'Lya gasped in horror.

"That is the problem," Mrs. Norris said while placing a reassuring hand on Marziah's shoulder. "How can we allow a half human to fit in with our family? It is shocking and disgraceful. What if a young suitor were to dine with us and he were to fancy Femili *instead* of Marziah or Ju'Lya? It would be an embarrassment to both us and him. No, we must do our best to make sure her parentage is always known. We must make it clear to Femili and everyone that comes in contact with her that she is part human. She can never be made to feel or believe that she is part of acceptable AiJalonian society. In fact, I suggest releasing one of your personal service droids to me and Mr. Norris and letting Femili be the replacement."

"Wouldn't that be rather inefficient?" Comte Thomas protested.

"You can think of it as a help to Mr. Norris and myself. We could certainly use it. I have been meaning to purchase another droid as we only have three at the moment, but you know how tight our budget is. I feel this is the perfect solution."

"I was not asleep," Comtesa Berzam said suddenly as she very obviously jolted awake.

"Of course, you weren't, my dear," her husband said as he patted her gently on the top of the head.

"Sister," Mrs. Norris said quickly, "we were just discussing how nice it would be if you and Comte Thomas would generously donate one of your service droids to me in order to assist me in the care of dear, old Mr. Norris."

"Donate a service droid? Well, what on AiJalon would we do instead?"

"Wouldn't you rather the interaction with a living being instead of a cold robot? Your niece Femili could easily and capably fill that void."

"Well, I suppose that's true."

"Then it is settled," Mrs. Norris said energetically. "I will take a service droid with me and Femili will take its place."

Comte Thomas couldn't help but wonder why she didn't just have Femili live with her at the rectory which he thought was the original plan.

***

She was his cousin. The first woman he had ever been attracted to in his life turned out to be his close family relation. What kind of evil twist of fate was this? Edwin was seventeen and had never had feelings for a woman. It had become a point of contention with his older brother who by the same age had been able to boast of two romantic affairs.

Publicly, Edwin had blown off the remarks. He was only seventeen. He was still rather young. And while it was normal for girls to marry at this age, boys typically waited a bit longer. Privately, however, he too wondered about his preferences. Why had no woman ever stirred his heart like he'd read about in Engorian romance novels? Since no man had ever stirred him either, he didn't consider that he was homosexual. Rather, he thought of himself as possibly asexual. He thought he would never develop romantic feelings for anyone, thus, he thought he would be a perfect priest or minister.

That was until he had laid eyes on Femili. Then all at once, every single, pious thought completely left his mind. Maybe he was not destined for a life of celibacy after all.

But alas, the woman who had awakened these feelings in him turned out to be his cousin. And not a distant cousin. The daughter of his mother's twin sister. The only way she could be more closely related was if she was herself his sister.

Edwin spent the rest of the day praying ... to several gods ... for answers, direction, help— anything. What exactly was he supposed to do in this situation?

He started by trying to completely ignore her. If she wasn't there, he couldn't have feelings for her. *If I don't see her, I can forget her.* He could just pretend she didn't exist. Or so that was what he thought. But that logic had several flaws. First, it was exceptionally difficult to ignore someone when they lived in the same house as you did. Though Mansfield Park was quite large, it was still impossible to completely avoid her. Secondly, even if he never saw her again, the vision of her when they first met was still indelibly engraved on his mind and heart. He still kept her handkerchief. Though he refused to look directly at it, his eyes daily glanced at the desk where it lay waiting to be held again.

***

There weren't many things Femili could say she honestly liked about Mansfield Park. Sure, it was a grand old house, she had plenty of food, and the workload was similar if not a bit lighter than what she had on Minnith. But the constant belittling from her cousins Marziah and Ju'Lya and even her Aunt Norris was beginning to test the amount of Gaion's grace she could spare. Some days she would much rather be on Minnith because even though she was poor, she at least was loved.

Her habit of retreating to the conservatory to read next to a Poplin tree native to Minnith was the highlight of her day. Unfortunately, her cousins quickly learned of her hiding spot and continued to torment her.

"I bet you don't even know the founding families of AiJalon or the succession of Kings and Queens," Marziah said one day almost two months after her arrival.

Femili looked up from her book, confused. "Are you talking to me?"

"Of course she is. Who else would she be talking to?" Ju'Lya asked.

"You, perhaps," she said to Ju'Lya. Femili's tone had no sarcasm or vitriol in it, but it still made both Marziah and Ju'Lya feel quite stupid as it was indeed possible that Marziah was addressing Ju'Lya.

"Well, no. I am talking to you, Femili," Marziah said. "Do you know the names of the twelve founding families or the succession of Kings and Queens?"

Femili looked confused. "Why would I know that? I grew up on Minnith. Do you happen to know the succession of the Orthodox Minarin priesthood?"

"What is that?" Marziah asked.

"In the Orthodox Minarin religion, which is the most populous on Minnith, there is a succession of head priests. It is usually passed down from father to son, but there have been some fascinating usurpations. How about you study the succession of Minarin head priests and I will study the succession of AiJalonian Kings and Queens?"

Marziah and Ju'Lya were at a loss for words. They had attempted to humiliate and embarrass Femili, but this human child of fifteen seemed unflappable and it was downright infuriating.

Unprepared for a secondary attack, both girls retreated to their rooms. Suddenly, Femili heard clapping.

"Bravo, young cousin," Thom said from the other side of the conservatory. Femili hadn't even realized he was there. "My sisters were just trying to intimidate you with their superior knowledge. Hopefully, they will realize that their knowledge is not, in truth superior—just alternative to yours." Thom took a sip of his wine then shook his head. "Probably not. They are a spoiled pair. They would fare much better in life if my father provided them with less in the way of possessions and more in the way of his time."

Femili had no idea why Thom was being so open with her. Maybe it was the wine talking.

"And my mother." He sighed. "Mother is Mother. She has a rather fragile constitution and cannot be stressed with the burden of actually raising children. But she does look quite lovely beautifully dressed and sitting on a sofa." He smiled, putting Femili somewhat at ease. "What about you, dear cousin? Did you spend a lot of time with your parents on Minnith?" he asked.

Femili nodded. "More than you can probably imagine. All twelve of us lived packed together in a home with only three rooms. Our entire home could fit in the parlor of Mansfield Park."

"Is that so?" he asked. Femili didn't understand the hint of skepticism in his voice. Did he think she was lying to him?

Femili pointed to his glass. "Do your parents know you drink? Are you not still underage?"

"The drinking age was recently changed. Now it is when you marry or when you turn twenty," he said as he twirled the brightly colored liquid around in his glass.

"But you're nineteen…and single," Femili said confused.

"Indeed, I am." He clinked an imaginary glass with her then finished his drink in one gulp.

"O…kay…" she said slowly still not quite knowing what to make of her cousin Thom. He was so different from his brother. Thom was a large man with a foreboding and muscular presence. In truth, he looked much older than nineteen which is why no one would suspect he was underaged and drinking. Edwin on the other hand had a lean physique. And his curly hair made him look more like an adorable puppy than any potential threat. She missed those sweet brown eyes that she saw for the first time in Cosmo. There was something so comforting about them.

Femili stood to leave then said, "Have you seen Edwin at all? I know he rarely makes an appearance but I don't think I've seen him at all three days."

"He's probably off praying somewhere."

"Right." So, one brother illegally drank in public while the other hid away to pray. She sighed. Would she ever understand AiJalonians?

Chapter 5

The first event of any consequence at Mansfield Park after Femili joined the family was the death of Mr. Norris which happened about six months after her arrival. Femili thought it would be a more notable event. She had never had anyone in her family die, but she imagined it would cause more of a disturbance than merely Mrs. Norris joining them for breakfast thirty minutes later than usual.

As it turned out, breakfast and dinner were the worst parts of the day for Edwin.

The morning of his uncle's death was no different. Edwin could usually find some reason to be away from the home for mealtimes, but for some reason his mother insisted on eating together for breakfast and dinner even though she routinely overslept for the former and fell asleep during the latter.

During mealtimes, Femili was obligated to bring the food to the table as if she were no more than a slave. It was utterly ridiculous. Living beings hadn't been used as servants on this planet in a hundred years. He knew all too well why they were doing this. They were intimidated by her. And for good reason too. If Femili wasn't half human, she would be the most sought-after woman in the archipelago, perhaps in the nearest several archipelagos.

The morning of Uncle Norris's death, his sisters apparently felt particularly emboldened. Mother was sleeping, Mrs. Norris hadn't arrived, Father was preparing for yet another journey off planet and Thom was ... well, Thom was doing whatever it was Thom did for days at a time. No one in the family actually knew. In any case, Marziah and Ju'Lya took it upon themselves to torment their cousin.

"What are you doing?" Ju'Lya asked as Femili sat down to eat breakfast.

Femili looked around confused. "I am going to eat my breakfast."

"At this table?" Marziah asked as if the two of them had planned this ambush.

"Well, yes."

"Do not you think you should eat somewhere else?" Ju'Lya asked.

"Why would ... ?" Femili paused and took a deep breath. "Every day after I serve you, I then sit down and eat as well. It has been this way for more than six months."

"It should change," Marziah said. "It is completely unacceptable to have a human sit at the table with us."

Everyone subconsciously looked over to where Thom usually sat, waiting for him to interject "half human" as he always did when anyone called Femili human. But he wasn't there. "Anyway, what if someone sees you here?" she continued.

"Someone like whom?" Femili asked.

"A single, wealthy AiJalonian just bought Sanrik Isle," Ju'Lya said. "What if he plans to court one of us? He would be disgusted by your presence and we would miss out on a potential marriage mate."

At this point, Edwin wanted to jump to the defense of Femili, but he did not trust himself. He was afraid that if he defended her too fiercely, all in the room would learn of the feelings he had for Femili that had not subsided in the least in the six months of her presence. So, instead he stayed silent and watched as her normally lively spirit slowly withered before his eyes.

Femili glanced outside the window. "It really is a lovely morning. I think I will go enjoy my breakfast in the garden."

Edwin tried to hold in his feelings. Maybe acknowledging the fact that she was half human would help solidify the fact that they could never be together. She was his cousin and she was human. Those two things should be enough to forget about her, right? To not care about the hurt he saw in her eyes as she left the room? No, somehow it wasn't enough.

"Was that really necessary?" Edwin asked his sisters moments later.

"What?" they asked in unison. They were both honestly confused as to why Edwin would care.

"Jealousy is not a flattering accessory."

"Jealousy?" Marziah asked. "Are you suggesting we are jealous of her?"

"How ... Why would we be jealous of a barbaric, ignorant half-breed like her?" Ju'Lya added.

"I don't care what breed half of her is, she is more AiJalonian than the two of you put together." He pushed his food away and went to find Femili in the garden.

***

Comte Berzam took a break from preparing for his trip to Pentauch to visit Mrs. Norris at the abbey on his property and pay his respects for the death of his friend Mr. Norris. He entered the small residence and felt a tinge of pain. He would miss his friend, but he was happy that he was able to afford him a comfortable existence for the final fifteen or so years of his life. At the same time, he was able to provide companionship for his wife's sister. He felt good with himself the way he had been able to help his wife's family. And now he would be able to continue doing that. After offering his condolences, he asked Mrs. Norris, "So when shall we send Femili over?"

Mrs. Norris looked utterly confused. "Send Femili over?"

"Yes, have you thought about where her room will be? Also, I expect that the service droid will be returned to Mansfield proper. But there is no rush."

"Forgive me, Comte Berzam, but I have no idea what you are talking about?"

Comte Berzam now looked equally confused. "When Femili moved in six months ago, you said she was not able to live here at the abbey because Mr. Norris was ill. Now that he is gone, that is no longer a concern. I also thought that she would be quite a comfort to you in your time of mourning. I know she has been a great comfort to my wife."

"I really have no idea how you could have come to such a conclusion. Never has such a thought entered my mind. I am a new widow. How on AiJalon could I care for a child at this stage in my life and in such a small residence and on such a small income? And for you to be bringing this up so soon after my husband's death! Really, Comte Berzam, I had no idea how insensitive you could be."

Comte Berzam couldn't quite decide if he was offended or hurt by these comments. He had no intention of being insensitive so he was hurt by the insinuation, but he was also offended. How could she even accuse him of such intention after all that he had done for her?

"Mrs. Norris, did I somehow misunderstand our agreement?"

"Truth be told, I don't remember ever entering into any such agreement. You are the one with the means and ability to care for the child. I feel placing her here at the abbey would be putting both her and myself at a disadvantage. Would you not agree? Besides, you yourself said that she has been such a comfort to your wife. Who are we to deprive your wife of such comfort? Really, if you honestly think this through, I am sure you would agree that it is for the best if Femili stay right where she is at Mansfield Park. And speaking of Mansfield Park, I do believe I am late for breakfast. Shall we?" Mrs. Norris started walking toward the door, leaving Comte Berzam with no recourse but to follow her.

***

"Femili," Edwin said when he found her.

"Well, hello there, my elusive cousin," she said, smiling brightly. How could she be so happy at a time like this?

Her smile was infectious, however, and somehow, he couldn't help but smile as well while trying fervently to keep his heart rate to a reasonable speed.

"Elusive? What do you mean by that?" he asked, attempting small talk.

"Oh, do you need help defining AiJish words? Shall I say it for you in Engorian, or Minnith, or perhaps ancient Ai?"

"You speak Ancient Ai?"

She nodded. "My mother taught me a little. I am not very good at it, though."

"Maybe I could help you practice."

"I'd like that."

"So why do you call me elusive?" he asked in Ancient Ai.

Femili paused to gather her thoughts and figure out how to make the correct response in the admittedly difficult language. Though, for some reason, she found it much easier to speak Ancient Ai now that she was on AiJalon. She wondered if that was just a psychological side effect of being on her mother's home planet.

"You have not said more than two words to me since we met at the station six months ago. Why?" she asked in near-perfect Ancient Ai.

Edwin felt his face flush. It was a good thing he was dark-skinned so that she wouldn't be able to tell how flustered he was. Now it was his turn to pause and formulate a response. He couldn't think of one that would make sense so he instead focused on correcting her ancient Ai grammar.

"Thank you for the grammar lesson," she said in AiJish when he was finished. "I truly appreciate it. But you still didn't answer my question."

It was at this moment he hated his AiJalonian genetics the most. His biochemistry made it extremely difficult to lie without certain obvious reactions in his body. His reaction to falsehoods was stronger than most. His sister Marziah, for example, had taught herself to control her symptoms and only suffered a small rash on her right elbow. As long as she forced herself not to touch it, she could get away with lying. Edwin, on the other hand, suffered nausea, a piercing pain in his head, and a full body rash complete with itching. Lying just wasn't worth the physical pain which was why he never did it. But he would perhaps need to make an exception in this case.

"When I met you, I did not know you were my relation," he began slowly while trying to find the most truthful and least embarrassing words possible. "Now that I know you are my family and that you live with us, I have decided to treat you like my sister. And I do not like my sisters very much."

Femili began choking on her fial porridge made from the leftovers of her cousins' breakfast. Though it was made from leftovers, it was still more substantial and tastier than anything she had eaten on Minnith. Edwin rushed to her side to pat her on the back. Suddenly, the choking turned into laughing.

"Dear Gaion, Edwin! You are hilarious. I can't believe you've deprived me of this humor for these last several months. Honestly, this is the first time I've laughed since I've been here."

He noticed tears welling in her eyes. He literally sat on his hands to prevent himself from wiping them away when they fell.

"If I have made you laugh, then why are you crying?"

Femili blinked away the tears and tried to compose herself. "I don't mind being ridiculed and criticized here. I am used to it by now. And it's easier to bear, I suppose, because I realize how, well, *unhappy* everyone here is, in their own ways.

"Because of our financial situation, living in constant misery was the norm when I was on Minnith. But even in all that pain, I still found reasons to laugh, especially with my brother Wynn and my sister Benie. I suppose laughing for the first time reminded me of how much I miss them." Femili turned to him and added. "I would love it, Edwin, if you would not distance yourself from me. If you could try to make me laugh as much as possible, I would be eternally grateful."

What could he do? There was nothing he could do in this situation as he stared into her beautiful eyes and heard her sweet voice mention the word love in the same sentence as his name. Edwin was convinced that he would be headed to hell for merely the thoughts that were entering his head in her presence. But he would have to worry about that later. Right now, he was determined to do everything in his power to make sure she was happy.

Maybe if his pursuit of her happiness kept reminding her of her brother and sister then he would be safe.

His stomach twisted as he felt his breakfast staging a revolt.

If she kept thinking of him as a brother, maybe eventually one day he could see her as a sister.

Edwin fought hard to keep his expression clear and unaffected. An obviously failed attempt as he noticed Femili's brow furrow in concern. Hmm, it seemed lying to himself was still lying and his body was having the same violent reaction.

He swallowed hard trying to keep the vomit at bay while at the same time feeling his body sway to the side. The last thing he remembered was Femili calling his name.

Chapter 6

Femili stared at Edwin as he lay in his bed, wondering what on AiJalon could have made him pass out like that. They were having an innocent conversation about the potential for Edwin to be the go-to person for a good laugh. Something that she missed from her brothers and sisters. Edwin hadn't even responded before he dry heaved a few times then passed out cold.

She was at a loss as to what could be the reason. But she desperately wanted to find out. For the first time in six months, she felt like she wasn't just existing in Mansfield Park, but she felt like she could be happy one day.

Femili remembered seeing him for the first time at Mansfield Park after they had met at the station with Madame Noonan. She remembered feeling beyond relieved that he was there. They had had such a great conversation at the station that she had known they would be fast friends. But then he'd proceeded to completely ignore her once they had met again. Honestly, Edwin's behavior hurt her much more than anything Marziah and Ju'Lya could do. Femili could handle those two. They were just spoiled, insecure children. Being the oldest of ten, she had observed and dealt with her fair share of spoiled, insecure children. But Edwin was different. She wanted ... she wanted ... She actually was not sure what she wanted from him.

Thankfully, there was still a medical droid at Mansfield Park. Femili was not expected to take on that role as well. As the droid examined Edwin and ran tests, she was able to just stare at him. He certainly was beautiful. His deep, dark skin and sharp features were softened by a general sweetness. One look from him felt like a warm hug. She wanted to tussle his curly hair which was kept much longer than most AiJalonian men. It was an odd sensation she felt in his presence.

She wondered if he had any courting prospects. He was only seventeen and the second son so it was possible that he hadn't even begun to have those thoughts. On AiJalon, the oldest son inherited half the estate with the other half being evenly divided among the remaining children. Thus, the best situation for family unity on the planet was to only have two children. But as it was, Edwin, Marziah, and Ju'Lya would have to split fifty percent of Comte Thomas's estate three ways. Femili wasn't sure how much that would be, but she was quite sure it was not enough for Marziah and Ju'Lya's taste. They had already begun seeking out rich men from surrounding islands as prospective husbands to supplement their income.

For Edwin, it would be more complicated. He might have a hard time finding a mate given that his income would not be extravagant. Would he have enough financial assets to make a union with him enticing? Would he marry someone with more money than him so he could live comfortably? Or would he marry for love? The more important question at the moment, however, was why did she care?

"What happened?" Edwin asked as the stimulant given by the medical droid finally took effect.

"You passed out," Femili responded.

"Oh." Edwin suddenly remembered the circumstances of his downfall and silently prayed that she wouldn't repeat an inquiry into his feelings or his behavior towards her. He was now sure he could no longer lie to himself or to her. He was attracted to her. He wanted her. He loved her. He would just have to accept that or risk vomiting and passing out every time he told himself otherwise. Edwin hoped and prayed that somehow, slowly, he could see her in a different light. As a sister and not a lover.

"Since you are feeling better," she said, helping him to sit up, "how about we finish our conversation? Will you help me? Will you continue to make me laugh as much as you can?"

"I will do whatever you want me to do," he answered truthfully.

"Where is the medical droid?" they heard Aunt Norris yell from downstairs.

Both Femili and Edwin followed the droid to where it was being summoned only to find a bloodied and battered Thom Berzam stumbling through the front door.

"What happened?" Femili asked.

"I had a bit of an accident," Thom slurred. Femili couldn't tell if he was drunk or had lost feeling in his face from his multiple injuries.

"Edwin, brother. I am so sorry," Thom began. "I crashed your guster."

"Don't worry about that now. Let's get you fixed up." Edwin helped his brother to the sofa in the parlor.

"Tell the droid no Dexafinlen," Thom said when the medical droid started examining him. "Jason already gave me morphine for the pain and additional Dexafinlen will give me nasty side effects."

"Who or what is Jason and morphine?" Aunt Norris asked.

"Morphine is a painkiller common among humans," Femili answered. "I don't know who or ... what Jason is."

"Of course, the human would be familiar with their common illicit drugs," Aunt Norris said.

"Half!" Thom yelled then giggled. "She is half human. Must I always correct you people?"

"What is wrong with him?" Comte Berzam said upon entering the parlor.

"He is injured," Edwin said. "We don't know why or how.

And he was given a drug that I think is making him behave oddly."

"Drugs? Were you on drugs when you crashed your brother's guster?"

"Actually, not," Thom said between giggles.

"How could you be so irresponsible? That was a Galvin class guster. There are only a handful of them left on the planet. It was part of your brother's inheritance."

"It really doesn't matter, Father," Edwin said. "Let's just make sure he's okay."

"It does matter. By law, I can only split your inheritance a certain way. That guster was meant to even things out. Now what am I supposed to do?"

"Look at him!" Thom yelled suddenly. "Look at how good-looking my brother is. He will marry rich and be set for life."

"Thom, I demand to know where you have been, what you have been doing, and what kind of drugs you have been taking this instant."

Unfortunately, Comte Berzam would have to wait for any answers as Thom immediately fell unconscious.

After the medical droid made an initial diagnosis, Edwin helped Thom to his room and Femili took it upon herself to be his personal nurse.

Thom's injuries weren't too serious, just cuts and bruises that the medical droid patched up as well as a dislocated shoulder. But in caring for her cousin, she noticed that he had many other scars and injuries as well.

"You can go ahead and ask," Thom said when his medication had worn off and he noticed her staring at him. "Of course, you may ask and I may choose not to answer."

"You're a very odd boy."

"Well, that wasn't a question at all. It was more of a statement, but I will answer it anyway I suppose." He cleared his throat then said, "Correct. I can take 'odd'. It's better than idiot. But what I lack in knowledge, I make up for in instincts. And my instincts are telling me that there is more to your story Femili Primme." He tried to stand and instantly regretted it.

"You probably shouldn't do that. You are going to be dizzy for a while."

"Right," he said, sitting back down.

Femili selected her next set of words carefully. She was extremely curious as to what her cousin had been up to and wanted to ask him directly. Given that
AiJalonians were practically incapable of lying,

it seemed like an easy thing to do.

But because of their inability to lie, they had also developed very artful ways of answering questions without giving away any useful information. Plus, at any time, Thom could just choose not to answer at all.

"So," she said after a few moments, "are you ever going to explain why you were on Capernica? They don't call it a planet of thieves for no reason."

"How did you ... "

"You have a Bandit Brand on your wrist meaning you were robbed."

Thom's eyes enlarged in shock. She knew she was right.

"And you didn't crash Edwin's guster, did you?" she added.

"How did you know that?"

"That one I didn't know. It was just a guess. But I suppose I am correct."

She sat next to the bed and continued. "That was the real reason for the drugs you were on, wasn't it? So that you could lie about what really happened to the guster."

Thom crossed his arms. Curiosity suddenly triumphed over his fear of revealing the truth.

He had to hear more from his little cousin. "Please continue your analysis."

"Morphine doesn't react with Dexafinlen under the proper dosage and a medical droid would be able to figure that out. Dexafinlen does cause deadly side effects with any number of psychotropic drugs which would be needed to allow an AiJalonian to lie convincingly and without physical side effects."

"Well done, Miss Femili Primme. Well done. But tell me, how does a half-human, half-AiJalonian teenager who grew up on Minnith know all of this?"

Femili stared down at the ground. She should have made up a believable lie like she had read it in a book or something. The truth scared her more than the lie and part of her hoped her mysterious cousin could help her figure things out. "Honestly, I don't know," she said.

"If I believed in Engorian magic I would swear you were some sort of witch."

"Who is a witch?" Edwin said, suddenly entering the room

Thom and Femili stared at each other, neither one of them wanting to let Edwin know what they were talking about.

"Why don't you take our little cousin for a walk?" Thom said, skillfully redirecting the conversation and capitalizing on what he had observed about his brother's interest in her. He wondered if Edwin was curious about her parentage as well.

"Yes, how about a walk around the lake?" Femili said while grabbing Edwin's hand. It wasn't until they were all the way to the lake that she realized she was still holding his hand.

"Oh, sorry," she said releasing him.

Edwin looked down at his hand and breathed probably for the first time since they left Thom's room together. Had he really not touched her since the spaceport in Cosmo six months ago?

"I take it from the way you speak that your brother Wynn is whom you miss most from Minnith," he said desperate to start an innocent conversation to take his mind off of her touch.

Femili nodded. "I miss all of my siblings of course, but Wynn was my truest companion."

"Have you talked to him since you have come to Mansfield?"

Femili shook her head. "I don't have the means to."

"What do you mean? Have my parents not afforded you your own personal TelEx?"

"Oh, yes, they have generously given me one, but communication on Minnith is very difficult. My family cannot afford a device to receive a transmission and even if they could, the atmosphere around the planet makes intergalactic communication very difficult and expensive."

Edwin thought for a moment. "What about a handwritten letter?"

"Like with ink and paper? How adorably antique!"

Edwin could see how delighted she was at the prospect. Her eyes brightened and her smile was even more beautiful than usual.

"Do you think you'd really be able to find paper and ink?"

Yes, tracking down paper and ink would be a challenge. A challenge he was up to for two reasons: it would distract him momentarily and it would bring her joy. Was he doomed to spend the rest of his life like this? Seeking things that would make her happy even though what would make *him* happiest would be to be with her? If that was his fate, he could learn to cope.

Chapter 7

AiJalon had been in existence for many thousands of years that some thought it was the oldest planet in the galaxy. Even AiJalonians who worshipped on Minnith believed that AiJalon was the first planet that Gaion created. In any case, at one point it was a completely pure and pious planet as well, almost like Minnith. But over the recent centuries, many other cultures began to pour their influence in and dilute the true AiJalonian tenets of cleanliness of mind, body, and spirit.

The biggest change in AiJalonian history came when humans tried and failed to colonize the planet. They arrived in large, clunky, antiquated spaceships after their carnivorous existence completely decimated their own planet.

They actually set out to conquer many planets in the galaxy. While they had a measure of success on planets like Tentor, their efforts were a complete failure on AiJalon. The magnetic core on AiJalon allowed the natives to have complete control of any weapon that was brought to the planet. Thus, attacks from enemies proved to be fruitless as AiJalon always had the advantage.

Femili wondered if the magnetic core of AiJalon also had effects in the biochemistry of AiJalonians as well. It would be the only way to explain what had been happening to her since she had come to the planet.

Since she moved to AiJalon, Femili had been plagued with odd dreams. Dreams that played as if they were previews from a Globe Box into a life that wasn't hers. She saw herself talking to people, going to places, and doing things that were completely unfamiliar to her.

Most nights the dreams merely played out as if she were watching someone else's life. Someone that looked exactly like her.

While weird, they were bearable. But other nights were different. Some of the events she saw were truly frightening and caused her to cry and scream in her sleep. Unbeknownst to her, it was loud enough to wake her cousins. Well, one of them at least.

"Are you all right?" Edwin asked one night about seven months after she came to live at Mansfield Park. She had awakened to see him sitting next to her.

Instead of answering, Femili flung herself into his arms, clinging to him as if her life depended on it. He wrapped his arms around her and held her tightly as she cried. "Femili, what's wrong?"

"I don't know! I don't know!" She clung to him even more tightly.

"Shh, it's okay. Just cry," he said. "I'm here for you."

And cry she did. She didn't even understand exactly why she was crying. She just knew she was frightened and unsure of what was happening to her. That night, she fell back asleep in his arms. When she woke the next morning, he was still in her room, sitting next to the bed.

"Edwin, I'm so embarrassed."

"Don't be. I'm just glad I came this time."

Femili was confused. "This time?"

"This happens every month on the third. It's like clockwork. You scream in the night."

"Really?"

He nodded. "Usually, I just send a droid to wake you up. This time I decided to check on you myself. I'm glad I did."

"I am sorry to have disturbed you. I really don't know ... I don't understand ... I—"

"You do not have to explain what you do not understand."

They both fell silent for a moment.

"Hey, I have an idea," Edwin said with a change of tone. "Since this only happens on the night of the third, let's start a tradition. On the third day of every month, we won't go to sleep. We can talk, read, look at the stars, swim— whatever it takes so that you won't have night terrors."

Could she dare accept? To have someone there to chase away the nightmares and the awful questions left behind was tempting. Having Edwin close would certainly ease her mind, even if it left her heart even more vulnerable to him than it already was. She took a deep breath and decided to take the risk. Anything would be better than seeing this images again.

And so, the plan was born.

"What is going on?" Thom asked Edwin as he saw him exiting Femili's room. Thom was on his way for an early morning swim and ran into his younger brother.

"Nothing. Nothing. Absolutely nothing is going on. I didn't spend the night in there. Well, I did, but I was sitting in a chair and she was in the bed."

Thom looked at his brother strangely. "Why are your words so fast-paced?"

"Am I talking fast? I didn't realize. Maybe I am just tired."

"Wouldn't that be a reason for talking slowly?"

"Oh, yes, perhaps."

Thom continued staring at his brother without saying anything. He had found over the years that this was the best way to get a confession out of Edwin.

"Femili had a night terror and I went to comfort her," he said finally.

"Oh. Why didn't you say so? Thank you for taking care of her. Someone should." Thom glanced around the hallway for a moment, making sure all other bedroom doors were closed. Then he pulled Edwin away from Femili's door and whispered, "Have you noticed anything strange about our cousin?"

"Strange? What do you mean?" Edwin asked.

"Doesn't she seem not very human at all? And she is also extremely smart and perceptive."

"Are you saying she's too smart to be part human?"

"No, that's not ... " Thom sighed in frustration. He wasn't sure what he was saying either. There was something not right about Femili and he just couldn't put it into words exactly. "You don't find it strange that she knows so much about everything when she grew up on Minnith? Minnith! It is a planet of priests, for Gaion's sake."

"I plan on being a priest one day, Thom. What's wrong with that?"

"Nothing, I'm not ... Oh, never mind." Thom shook his head. "Just keep an eye on her. Take care of her. And let me know if you see anything else that is ... strange." He walked away frustrated.

What was he getting at? Edwin wondered.

***

It was probably during one of these stay-awake-all-night events that Femili fell for her cousin. She didn't intend for it to happen. Honestly, who would purposely fall in love with their cousin? But it happened. He was the one who made her smile, comforted her when she was sad, protected her when she was scared. He was always there for her. What else did she expect to happen? She took solace in the fact that it was a hopeless, one-sided infatuation that wouldn't (and couldn't) ever come to fruition. Little did she know how soon that would change.

Chapter 8

Femili had read in ancient books that on some planets, turning eighteen was some sort of milestone. It meant that the person was an adult and was met with celebration and new freedoms. For Femili, there was no such thing. Her eighteenth birthday came and went with absolutely no fanfare. In fact, on AiJalon, the milestone should have been when she turned sixteen. According to tradition, she should have had a summit in her honor introducing her to the community as an eligible marriage mate.

No such summit occurred for Femili, however, even though she had heard about the summits given in Marziah's and Ju'Lya's honors before she had arrived.

In fact, instead of one summit, Marziah actually had a series of summits that lasted over a week.

Femili had no reason to be jealous of Marziah. She wasn't especially attractive, or bright, or talented. She seemed miserable all the time and the way she constantly tormented Femili seemed to just add to her misery instead of subtract from it. But there was one area in which Femili was slightly jealous. Marziah had begun to court a wealthy island owner named Mr. Rushworth. She wasn't jealous that the man was wealthy, but merely that Marziah was able to openly court someone. Femili too wanted to love and be loved. But the person she wanted was out of reach for her.

Being able to openly court someone didn't seem to make Marziah any happier of a person, however, even though this courtship had dragged on for well over a year. But then again, Femili wasn't sure if there was anything in the world that would actually make Marziah happy.

"What do you mean he proposed and you accepted?" Edwin asked at breakfast one morning after the engagement.

Marziah shrugged. "Yes, it was a couple of days ago, I think." She didn't seem too terribly affected one way or the other that she was about to be a married woman. It seemed like another natural, boring, and daily occurrence. Nothing special.

"And you are just bringing this up now? Isn't marriage like the endgame for you? I would think you would be proclaiming it from the rooftops," Thom said.

Marziah glared at her brother. "Aren't you the least bit embarrassed that I will be getting married before you?"

Thom shrugged. "No. Should I be?"

"It is different for men," Ju'Lya said. "Especially for the oldest. Thom can marry who he wants, when he wants, because he inherits half the estate. Perhaps Edwin is a little worried.

Edwin, for his part, was no longer listening to the conversation. Instead, his attention was focused on his cousin Femili.

"And what is the path for today?" Edwin asked as he helped Femili clear the breakfast dishes.

Femili smiled and sighed. "I think today, we should race to Pidan Falls, swim the length of the waterfall basin three times, race back, and then proceed with a duster race to the market."

"Really? Three times across the basin. I think you are giving yourself an unfair advantage. I don't know how a human is a better swimmer than I am but somehow you are."

"Half," Thom interjected. His seat was close enough to overhear the whispered conversation. "Half human."

"Gaion, Thom. I know," Edwin said, annoyed. "I'm just teasing her."

It was true. Edwin was just teasing. And Femili didn't mind when Edwin teased her about her humanity. She knew that with him, it was coming from a place of affection.

"So, when do we start?" Edwin asked.

Femili took the remaining dishes out of Edwin's hand and placed them in the machine. Then she took off her servant cape and handed it to him. "Now!" she yelled before sprinting out the door.

"That's cheating!" he yelled after her. He dropped the cape and started running to catch up.

"You know us humans," she yelled over her shoulder. "We're all cheaters!"

"Half! You're only half human!" he yelled.

"Where are they going?" Comte Thomas asked his eldest son as he saw Femili and Edwin run past them.

"It's their new thing," Thom said, not taking his eyes off of his TelEx. "A daily triathlon to see who is in better shape. If you ask me, it is just an excuse to be together away from the rest of the family."

"What did you say?"

Thom finally looked up. "Have you not noticed that those two are exceedingly close?"

Comte Thomas thought for a moment. He had noticed that Femili and Edwin were rather close but he had never thought anything of it. "What are you trying to say?"

"Nothing," Thom said, looking back down at his TelEx. "Has anyone ever done a DNA analysis on our little cousin?" he asked a few moments later.

"No, why would we?"

"No reason." Thom stood and stretched his aching muscles. He surely didn't want to alarm the family with his wild suspicions about Femili's parentage. His gut instincts kept telling him that his little cousin did not have a human father. Ultimately, would it really matter? She was still family. "How is the business on Pentauch? Do you need me to make a trip?"

"We can go together."

"Fine."

As expected, Femili made short work of the waterfall basin. There really was no explanation as to why she was so fast in water. Humans did not have a gill flap that allowed them to extract oxygen from the water like AiJalonians did. And though she was half AiJalonian, the gill flap gene was recessive. Before her, he had never met a mistura that had them. In any case, he was used to losing to her in swimming races.

Femili won their swimming competitions so often that today she was a little bored with it. Instead of quickly jumping out of the water and continuing to the duster race, she decided to wait behind the waterfall and enjoy the view. A few minutes later, Edwin joined her.

"Are you giving up?" he asked breathlessly. "Afraid you will lose to me?"

Femili just giggled at his unwarranted bravado. "Just sit with me for a while."

"Gladly."

This particular waterfall emptied into one of the two magnetic ponds of Mansfield Park which meant not only did it look beautiful, but each drop of water literally sounded like a note of soft music.

The sound of the falling water was a peaceful serenade that lulled them both into a state of serenity. Before they knew it, they had both dozed off next to each other.

About an hour later, Femili slowly blinked her eyes awake. She felt unseasonably warm, as if someone had wrapped her in a blanket. But it wasn't a blanket. It was a pair of arms. They were Edwin's arms and she was lying on his chest. How did they get into such an intimate position? However, it happened, she wanted to slip away from him before he woke up and they both became embarrassed.

Femili tried to slip out of his embrace, but the arms tightened around her. "Don't," he said softly. He was awake? And he was holding her tightly? While they were both in bodysuits? She turned her head towards him and noticed that he was staring down at her.

"Don't what?" Femili asked even though she already knew.

"Don't go."

Suddenly, she found it difficult to breathe. "Edwin, what are you doing?" she asked.

"I don't ... I don't know," he said, pressing his eyes closed again.

She didn't know either. All she knew was that it felt right being in his arms and lying on his chest. He was her cousin. Her cousin that had become closer than a brother. How could something so wrong feel so good?

Maybe this was a dream. Maybe she was still sleeping. She decided to at least pretend she was asleep as she let her hand explore his chest. Apparently, he was going to play along as well. He pulled her closer and caressed her cheek with his hand.

Why was he doing this? Why was this happening after all this time? Three years of her forcing herself to think of him as a brother. Three years of trying to cool the desire for him that had been glowing and here he was fanning the flame with one caress of his hand. She didn't know if she could take it. She would not be able to endure. This had to stop. Immediately. But it didn't. Instead, it intensified.

Edwin rolled over so that Femili was on her back and he leaned on top of her. "Fem," he whispered.

"Edwin."

"I'm sorry," he said before kissing her.

Why was he apologizing? Did he think she did not want this as well? If that was what he thought he was wildly mistaken.

This moment, tragic as it was, was something she had been dreaming about for years. What would his lips feel like? How would they taste? The answer to both those questions was better than she could have ever imagined.

But this tragic and ill-fated kiss would have to be the first and the last between them. It should have never happened in the first place. Poor Edwin would probably think he was going to hell for it.

"How did you...where did...how do you know about kissing?"

"I read about," he said still leaning over her. "Then I dreamt about it. And I think I've practiced it with you in my mind ten times a day for the past three years."

She was too shocked to speak. Three years. He had dreamed of kissing her for three years? Did he want her as much as she wanted him?

"I'm sorry," he said when she didn't say anything. He started to pull away from her. "I shouldn't have—"

Before he could finish his thought, she pulled him down into another kiss. If they were going to hell, they might as well make it worth the trip, she thought.

"We should stop," she said moments later.

"Yes, we should." But they didn't and instead began round three. Finally, almost an hour later, they were able to stay away from each other long enough to get a few words out.

"What do we do?" Femili asked, scooting as far away from Edwin as she could and still be heard under the waterfall.

"Gaion forgive us."

"He will. He will forgive us." She hugged her knees and dared not look at him. "He is a merciful god. As long as we never let this happen again."

"We have to pretend it never happened," Edwin said. "We have to beg for forgiveness and then pretend it never happened and never let it happen again."

"Agreed," Femili said. "It never happened." With that, she jumped through the waterfall and into the basin to make her way back to land.

Chapter 9

"I hate this repressed planet," Hin'Rik Crawly said as he paced the dining room of their rented house in Queli. He hated everything about his time on AiJalon even the residence they occupied which only contained ten rooms and four service droids for him and his sister. On their home planet of Engor, they lived in a veritable palace. In fact, it was a series of palaces along the oceanfront on the outskirts of the capital city. One for him, his father, his sister and even a palace for their favorite cousin. Now he was practically impoverished all because of a slight misunderstanding with the Engorian police.

His sister Meril sighed. "Yes, I know. You've made that very clear for the entire time we have been here."

"There is nothing to do. Everything is taboo; the so-called Ministry of Purity even restricts what you watch and what you listen to."

"What do you mean what you watch? Globe Boxes are illegal here. There is absolutely nothing to do here except make love and that is not approved." Meril began brushing her thin, long, black hair...again. It was the third time that day and the first sun wasn't even high in the sky. She suddenly envied AiJalonians who needed to spend several hours a day creating the intricate braiding patterns in their hair. At least it gave them something to do.

"Sister, you certainly are crude."

"Oh, you were thinking the same thing," she said with a huff. "Even if not the actual act, a bit of flirtation can be loads of fun and highly entertaining."

"Agreed. But they even have laws about flirtation on this planet."

Meril laughed. "They even have a name for it like a Contract Flirtation or Agreed Flirtation or something like that."

"It is absolutely insane," Hin'Rik said. "How much longer do we have on this forsaken planet?"

Meril looked at the brush in her hand and sighed. She was already done with her own hair…again. She signaled for her brother to sit in front of her so she could do his. Yes, she was bored enough to brush her brother's shoulder length hair and perhaps even style it in some sort of updo. "Father banished us from Engor for a year."

"It has been at least eight months hence, correct?"

Meril smirked as she tied his hair into a high ponytail. Though it was an unusual hairstyle for a man on this planet, there was still no chance of Hin'Rik being mistaken for a woman or anything of the sort. Her tall, muscular fair-skinned brother exuded manliness. He was dangerously masculine. It was part of the reason they both ended up banished. It was a long story that involved just a tiny bit of slightly illegal performances. "It's been less than a month, dear brother."

Hin'Rik groaned and whined in annoyance forcing Meril to have to redo his hair which was fine since they had a lot of time on their hands. "What are we going to do? Surely we'll die of boredom."

"I rarely agree with your exaggerations, but you might be close to accurate this time. So, I've thought of something we can do for a little entertainment."

Hin'Rik turned around and they sat facing each other. "How about a little competition?" she asked. She didn't even really need to ask. She knew he would be up for whatever.

"What did you have in mind?"

After handing him her TelEx, she said, "The Berzams are a wealthy family with two sons and two daughters. Their estate is just an island away."

"Two sons and two daughters. I see where this is going."

"Exactly. I mean look at the oldest son. He is absolutely scrumptious."

"Calm down, sister."

"The second son is attractive as well, but he wants to be a priest or something. He'll probably be a much more difficult conquest."

Hin'Rik nodded in agreement. "So what are the parameters?"

"Well, we have so much time, I think we should go all the way."

"Oh, scandalous."

"No, not that. Unless you really want to, of course. But with AiJalonians that would get uselessly complicated. I think just simple things will be enough for this group."

Meril's lips spread into a devilish grin. "We can devise a point system for things like hand-holding and kissing and so forth. And double points for both siblings. So, for example, if you kiss Marziah, it's ten points but if you kiss Ju'Lya afterwards it is an additional twenty points."

"It says here that Marziah is engaged. I should get twenty points for both."

"No way, Hin'Rik. You know women are easier than men in these situations. I'm the one who is going to have to fight against archaic societal norms of pious, virtuous women with zero sexual desires." Meril imitated vomiting.

"That is not necessarily true. I think we need to meet with them for an initial assessment and then we can determine a scoring system."

"Agreed."

That meeting took place the next day over afternoon tea. Unbeknownst to them, the entire Berzam clan was being assessed and evaluated. A price was being placed on each of their heads.

"It is so nice of you to pay us a visit," Comtesa Berzam said. "I am so sorry my husband and eldest son are not here to join us also. They are off planet for a few weeks."

"Well, we are new to the archipelago and wanted to get to know all of our neighbors," Meril said.

"How considerate of you," Mrs. Norris said. "Where did you say you are from?"

"We are on vacation from Engor for a year or so," Hin'Rik said.

"On vacation for a year?" Mrs. Norris asked, obviously impressed. She began doing the calculations in her mind. In order for them to be able to afford the estate they were renting in Queli for a year they had to be quite wealthy. "Are you also taking care of some business while you are on vacation? Comte Thomas often does this while in Pentauch. You know, mixing business with pleasure."

"I can assure you, we are here merely for pleasure," Meril said. Hin'Rik had to take a sip of tea in order to hide his sly grin.

Mrs. Norris liked this answer. It confirmed her suspicion and hope that they were from the elite Engorian class and not from the working class.

The young man was extremely good-looking, well-mannered, and independently wealthy. She would need to do a little more research into his background but so far it seemed he would be perfectly suited for her niece Ju'Lya.

"I would love for you to meet the children. Mrs. Norris, where are the children?"

"They took Mr. Rushworth's guster to the market, sister," Mrs. Norris said.

"Mr. Rushworth? Who is that?" Hin'Rik asked as if he didn't already know.

"Mr. Rushworth is my Marziah's fiancé. We are so elated to add him to the family," Comtesa Berzam said, stifling a yawn.

"Oh, how wonderful," Meril said with such sickeningly fake sweetness that her brother's stomach turned.

Mrs. Norris, on the other hand, was completely taken in by the false sincerity and began to wonder if the young woman would be a good match for one of her nephews. Honestly, she didn't know either of them too well. Thom was always jet-setting around the galaxy and even when he was home, he never let on what he was thinking or feeling very much.

Edwin seemed only interested in religion and Femili. She really couldn't decide which nephew she should pair with Meril, but since Thom was currently off planet, she decided to do a little matchmaking with Edwin.

Just then the guster arrived carrying Mr. Rushworth, Marziah, Ju'Lya, and Edwin.

Edwin was so relieved to be back at Mansfield Park. It was the first time he had spent a significant amount of time with his future brother-in-law and he was mentally exhausted. Karl Rushworth had to be the dumbest man he had ever been forced to hold in conversation. Mr. Rushworth had an odd obsession with flickerfish and talked about them incessantly. After just a few hours with him during that day, Edwin had already learned more about flickerfish than in all of his years of schooling. It was more than he ever wanted or needed to know. Why on AiJalon had Marziah agreed to marry him? Was it boredom? Desperation? He didn't know. He didn't really care. He just knew he would not be visiting them very often if at all.

"There is actually a species of it on Tentor that can survive on land for up to two days. Isn't that amazing?" Mr. Rushworth was saying as they entered Mansfield Park.

As soon as Edwin came through the door, he wanted to call for Femili. He needed a little bit of intelligent conversation to counteract the hours of flickerfish talk he had just endured. But then he remembered that he hadn't spoken to Femili since their encounter at the waterfall three weeks ago. His heart raced with excitement when he thought about it, but his mind also filled with unimaginable waves of guilt.

Edwin resisted the urge to call for her and instead entered the parlor where he found his mother and aunt sitting with two unknown guests.

"Oh, dear Edwin, perfect timing," his mother said. "Please meet our visitors, Heril and Minir."

"Hin'Rik and Meril," Mrs. Norris corrected quickly. "They are on holiday from Engor."

Edwin didn't know whether it was because he was so starved for company or whether they really were truly attractive, but in that moment, he thought the two Engorians were the loveliest beings he had seen in his life. As long as they didn't mention a flickerfish, that opinion would not be shattered.

"So pleased to meet you," Meril said with a ceremonial bow.

"Oh my," he heard from behind. He turned to see his sisters and Mr. Rushworth enter the room. All three were apparently stunned into paralysis. He expected the "Oh my" to come from one of his sisters in response to the sight of Hin'Rik, who was admittedly rather good-looking in an exotic sense with their fair skin, long straight hair and glowing eyes. But, instead, the expression came from Mr. Rushworth.

"What a lovely sibling pair," he said as he approached the two Engorians. "I can obviously see you are siblings. You look so much alike. Lovely. Just lovely. You remind me of a particular type of flicker—"

"Aunt Norris," Marziah said, interrupting her fiancé, "are you not going to introduce us?"

"Oh, yes. Of course. Hin'Rik Crawly, meet my young niece, Ju'Lya Berzam."

Marziah looked completely offended that she was not introduced first. But Aunt Norris knew exactly what she was doing.

Hin'Rik took Ju'Lya's hand in his and kissed it. A very Engorian thing to do.

An obviously jealous Marziah stuck her hand in front of his face in order for it to be kissed as well.

Hin'Rik gladly obliged. This seduction game was going to be easier than he thought as the two Berzam ladies sat on either side of him on the couch. Mr. Rushworth was left unaccompanied in the room as Meril began to converse with Edwin.

Comtesa Berzam fell asleep and Mrs. Norris silently sat back to observe her matchmaking.

"And where have you traveled to today?" Meril asked Edwin. "My brother and I have not been in the archipelago long and could use some guidance as to where to go for entertainment."

"Well, that depends on what you consider entertainment. I am afraid that AiJalon as a whole will not be nearly as enthralling as Engor. And Queli even less so."

"Oh, do not be so severe on yourself and your surroundings," Meril said flirtatiously. "I am quite enthralled right now."

Her comment was meant to amuse, entice, and intrigue him. It failed on all three counts. He seemed repulsed by her overt flirtation. She feared he would call the Ministry of Purity any moment.

Meril was not completely deterred, however. She had actually spoken the truth. She was enthralled with him at the moment. And it wasn't simply because Thom was not on the planet and thus, by default, Edwin would be the only chance she would have to earn points. There was something about Edwin's curt aloofness that was oddly attracting. She loved a challenge.

Meril took a sip of tea and wondered at what time of day would they bring out the stronger drinks.

"The first sun is setting," Hin'Rik said an hour or so later. "We should probably begin the journey back to our island."

"Oh, do stay for dinner," Mrs. Norris said, standing. She had been so delighted at how well the desired couples had been chatting that she didn't want it to end. Though she was put off a bit by how much Marziah spoke only to Hin'Rik, thus virtually ignoring her fiancé. She would have to address this with her later.

"Oh, no," Meril said sweetly. "We could not impose upon you on such short notice."

"It is not an imposition at all!" Mrs. Norris protested so loudly that it roused her sister.

"I was not asleep," Comtesa Berzam said as she jolted up.

"Of course, you weren't, sister. Why don't you help me convince our guests to stay for dinner?"

"We really are not able to accept the invitation tonight," Hin'Rik said. He and his sister needed to hurry back home and hash out the details of their seduction game now that they had made an initial assessment of the relevant parties.

Plus, it played in both their favors to always leave their objects of affection wanting more. "But," he added with a sly grin, "we would not be able to refuse an invitation for some time later this week."

"Of course, you can come back any time this week!" Ju'Lya said excitedly.

"Have some decorum," Mrs. Norris said to Ju'Lya in ancient Ai, hoping that the Engorian guests could not understand the language. Unfortunately for her, Ju'Lya could not understand it either.

"Do not fret," Hin'Rik said. "We have every wish to return. And return frequently." He kissed her hand again.

Hin'Rik and Meril walked back to their tobulin silently. Once they were comfortably inside Meril began.

"There is no way you are getting ten points for anything with either of those girls."

Hin'Rik smiled. "I knew you were going to say that. And I cannot say that I disagree."

"Of course, you cannot disagree. They practically unzipped your pants right there on the sofa."

"Now that would have been a sight."

"Meanwhile, Edwin is like the Wall of Tardil. How am I supposed to get anywhere with him?"

"Are you doubting your skills, sister?"

"Of course not. I am merely stating the obvious. That you have an unfair advantage. I swear to Gaion, I have never seen two more indecent AiJalonians in my life. I mean, even the ones who have lived on Engor for years show more morality than that."

Hin'Rik smiled. "I'm going to have so much fun with those two. It almost seems unfair."

"It *is* unfair," she said. "So how are we going to even the playing field?"

Chapter 10

Edwin could feel it. Even if it wasn't obvious from his aunt's comments over the past several days, he just felt it to be true. The fact that Meril Crawly was supposed to be a person of interest for him. She did have a few things in her favor. She was quite attractive, a true Engorian beauty. She was well-read and spoken, and most importantly, she was *not* his cousin, Femili. But she also had several things that worked against a recommendation in his mind. She was brazen, she often used Gaion's name in vain, and finally and most importantly, she was not Femili.

But he had resolved in his heart to try to see her as a prospect. She could prove to be a viable option given that he had no other prospects. It was worth a try. He even considered kissing her. There was no way kissing Meril Crawly would give him the same thrill kissing Femili gave him. But maybe part of that thrill was due to how forbidden it was. Perhaps kissing Meril would give a different but equally exciting sensation, but without the guilt. He was willing to try.

"We are so happy you could finally join us," Comtesa Berzam said. "I'm just sorry that my husband and eldest son are not here. They are off planet at the moment."

Meril and Hin'Rik gave each other a confused look. Didn't this woman already say this to them two days ago? Meril was tempted to take a swig of what the Comtesa was drinking. Whatever it was, it had to be quite strong.

"Where are the purple fial rolls?" Marziah asked, annoyed. "Did that girl not bring them out?"

"Girl? You give your servant droids genders?" Hin'Rik asked with a smile. He thought the idea of a female servant droid was quite comical on AiJalon.

Of course, there were many planets with male and female robots used for a variety of purposes, but that was another one of the concepts that was just too taboo for this planet.

"It's not a droid," Ju'Lya said. "We gave one of our servant droids away and our cousin does the work in its place."

"Why?" The question slipped from Meril's lips before she had time to think wisely. It was just such an illogical thing to do for so many reasons, she couldn't imagine why they would do such a thing.

"Well, because ... " Ju'Lya began but then realized she couldn't think of a way to phrase her response so that they all did not seem like monsters.

"It is because my half-human niece was destitute and needed a place to live and work. We so graciously provided both."

"I see," Meril said even though she really didn't.

Mrs. Norris had purposely had Femili set the dinner table before the guests arrived so that she wouldn't be seen by their guests. She didn't want to have to explain the situation. And now because of Marziah's thoughtlessness, the inevitable happened.

"Femili! Femili Primme, we need the rolls!" Marziah screamed.

Seconds later, Femili appeared and both Hin'Rik and

Meril instantly understood what was actually happening in the Berzam household. The Berzam cousin was absolutely stunning even in modest clothing. The Crawlys could barely imagine what she would look like if she was dressed in the elegant island gowns worn by her cousins Marziah and Ju'Lya.

It was immediately obvious that they had turned her into a servant in order to oppress her. It was like some AiJalonian version of Cinderella. Were they afraid she would be competition for Marziah and Ju'Lya? Meril smiled to herself for a moment at the thought. Poor Marziah and Ju'Lya would not stand a chance against this girl on looks alone. So unless she had some major personality flaw, Femili would definitely be the preference of anyone with eyes.

"Yes, cousin," the one called Femili said as she entered the room. "I have the rolls for you. I know they are your favorite so I made them fresh."

"You made them?" Hin'Rik asked. "With your own two hands?"

"Yes, of course. That is the way it's done where I'm from," Femili answered with a smile. Hin'Rik noticed that it was a genuine smile. There wasn't a hint of animosity or sarcasm. Was she truly happy with her situation? How was that even possible?

"How ... provincial," Hin'Rik said, still trying to wrap his head around the mystery that was Femili Primme. She looked like some sort of AiJalonian angel. If he were ever to read an AiJalonian textbook that spoke of the image of a perfect ancient beauty, he was sure a picture of Femili would be used. How was it that she was living as a half-human servant? It made no sense. "And where exactly are you from?"

"A paedor perhaps?" Marziah said with a snicker.

"You know full well she has never stepped foot in one of those," Edwin said, speaking for the first time that evening. And though he had taken the role of defending the pretty Femili Primme, he did not look up from his plate of food. Odd, Hin'Rik thought.

"When you insult me, you insult yourself. For I share your blood and your roof," Femili responded simply.

"I do not believe you have answered my question, Miss Femili Primme." Hin'Rik was not usually the one to diffuse a situation. In fact, he most often thrived on chaos and uncomfortable predicaments. But he truly wanted to know where she was from.

"Minnith," she said, setting the plate of purple fial rolls on the table.

"Ah, Minnith." He couldn't think of anything else to say. He really didn't know much about that planet except that it was filled with more churches than people. He really had no use for a society of priests and ministers. He found the entire concept of that planet tiresome and suppressive. Hin'Rik and Meril had vowed to never visit there.

"You may leave now, Femili," Mrs. Norris said.

"You couldn't pay me to stay," Femili said in a human language that both Hin'Rik and Meril recognized. They eyed each other and smiled.

"What did you say to me?" Mrs. Norris asked.

"Would you like me to leave or would you like me to answer? Which is more important?"

"Go. Just go," she responded.

"A wise choice as always, aunt."

Hin'Rik and Meril eyed each other again. Being that they were so close, they could practically tell what the other was thinking. They both felt she would be an exciting little addition to their game. Just how she would fit in, they weren't sure yet.

After dinner, the three prospective couples went for a walk. With droids walking in front and behind them providing soft lighting, it was supposed to be a romantic outing. For Edwin, it was just painful. Somehow, they ended up walking to the same waterfall where he had kissed Femili twenty-six days earlier. Had it really been twenty-six days? Some days he missed her so much it felt like it happened twenty-six years ago. Other days he missed her so much it felt like it happened twenty-six minutes ago. He was clearly going insane.

Edwin looked around suddenly and noticed that he was alone with Meril just steps away from the waterfall basin. Where had the others gone? He had been so lost in his thoughts that he really had no idea.

"How long has your cousin lived with you?" Meril asked. He really didn't want to talk about Femili. Not here especially. Not practically inches away from the scene of the crime.

Oh Gaion! He hadn't even thought about that aspect of it. Legally, it *was* a crime. It could be considered incest. They could be charged by the Ministry of Purity. He would probably just get a fine, but because Femili was half human, she would most likely be arrested and might be banished to a paedor afterwards. What had he done?

"Femili has lived with us for over three years. It's been so long that she is more like a sister than a cousin," he said more for himself than for Meril. It didn't help. Nothing did. He looked at Meril. He really looked at her. Was she beautiful? Most Engorians were, by the galaxy's standards anyway. But personally, he felt he could stare at this Engorian for a hundred years and not feel what he felt the first second he saw Femili.

He took a deep breath and tried to think logically. Why would Gaion let him feel these illicit feelings that were impossible to act on? He wouldn't. Maybe Meril was sent by Gaion to help him forget Femili. Based on how flirtatious she was at their first meeting, he felt she might be a willing replacement.

He turned to her and said, "Would you mind if I kissed you in the Engorian fashion?"

"Pehindyukominwen!" Meril exclaimed in Minnith. It was a word that roughly translated to 'Beat me till I swallow my own teeth and poop them out in my garden.' That damn planet of priests had the absolute best curse words. There was no other way to express how shocked she was that this shy, proper AiJalonian was actually making such a suggestion. "I must apologize," Meril said, trying to gain her senses. "I did not consider that you may know exactly what I said. You probably speak Minnith since your cousin is from the planet."

"Yes, she has taught me quite well." Edwin bit down on his own tongue hoping pain would help him forget the countless hours he spent alone with Femili while she taught him Minnith and he taught her ancient Ai.

"She seems very bright. I'm sure she's an—"

Interrupting her he said, "I would rather not talk about my cousin when I just asked a young woman for a kiss. May I kiss you now?"

"Yes, of course, I—"

Before she could finish her words, Edwin pressed his lips against hers. Too many thoughts ran through his head. Should he pretend he was kissing Femili or should he be purging her from his mind?

If the purpose of this little exercise was to get her out of his head, then thinking about getting her out of his head meant that she was still in there. This was not working.

He pulled away and stared at Meril. She wasn't his Femili. She didn't feel like her in his arms. She did not smell like her or taste like her. This kiss only convinced him that nothing and no one could replace Femili. "We should head back," he said, turning away from her.

Edwin was completely silent on the walk back to Mansfield Park which was perfectly all right with Meril. She had some things to work out in her mind. To her, life was always a game. People around her had to be assessed and leveraged for her advantage or pleasure. But suddenly she didn't know if she was a pawn or a player. What had just happened and what was going on with Edwin Berzam?

Meril continued to be lost in her mental calculations even on the tobulin ride with her brother back to their estate.

"I feel a little sorry for you, sister," Hin'Rik was saying. "I mean, not only do I have both Ju'Lya and Marziah, who each would probably kiss me just to make the other angry, but now I find out that there is a half-human cousin in the mix. Humans are just as passionate as Engorians. I am sure I can easily seduce her as well. Though don't you find Femili's looks a bit intriguing? I am no expert in genetics, but I really see no trace of human in her. In any case, I have three chances to your one. I am sure I will get one or more of these women to kiss me before Edwin is even willing to hold your hand."

"Edwin kissed me tonight."

"Pehindyukominwen!"

Chapter 11

Meril could not sleep that night. After Edwin had kissed her, she could not think of anything else. It wasn't as if it was her first kiss by any means. But it was the first kiss that she didn't expect. She honestly never saw it coming. And now she was consumed with the desire to understand exactly where it came from.

"What can you tell me about your cousin?" Meril asked Femili on her next visit to Mansfield Park. Based on her brief observations of the family, it was obvious that Femili was the only one worthy of interesting conversation.

As they visited the best waterfall of Queli, Meril

managed to get Femili alone for a few moments. Now she could question Femili about her the true object of her curiosity.

There were so many things Meril didn't know and didn't understand about Edwin Berzam. Her confusion made him incredibly sexy to her. There had never been a man she couldn't figure out in a manner of minutes. But Edwin Berzam was turning out to be an intricate web of contradiction upon contradiction. He admired the priestly society found on Minnith and even desired to enter the religious profession, but then he kissed her in a definitely non-religious way on practically their first meeting. Even if he didn't have the goal of being a Minnithite priest, he was still AiJalonian. Noble AiJalonians didn't even believe in kissing at all. It was a custom that they adopted from the human and Engorian cultures. How did he learn of it? Why did he do it? And why was he so damn good at it? She literally felt weak in the knees just thinking about it.

Meril, of course, could not ask these particular questions to Femili directly. But there were other things she could ask to better elucidate his motivations and his character.

Based on Meril's observation, Femili was the only

person in the Berzam household with any sense so she was clearly the one to ask.

"My cousin?" Femili asked.

Meril nodded.

"Do you mean Marziah, Ju'Lya, or perhaps Edwin?"

"Edwin, of course."

"Ah, I see," Femili said.

Meril blushed. At times it was a disadvantage being a fair-skinned Engorian instead of one of the darker ones. Her true emotions were often revealed in her complexion. Usually, it wasn't a problem because she rarely had true emotions. But now, feelings she had never felt before were beginning to develop. "Is it that obvious?" she asked.

Femili shook her head. "Not really. Don't worry. No one else in this house will discover your feelings. Except maybe Aunt Norris since she has been advocating for an attachment between the two of you from the beginning. So be careful of her."

"Thanks for the advice."

"So, my cousin Edwin. What can I say about him?" Femili sat down and stared at the calm, cool lake in front of her.

She had to calm her emotions and be rational about the

situation. Though Meril would not be the woman she would have chosen for Edwin, did that really matter? Meril, as morally loose as she might be, was still a better option for Edwin than herself, a family member. Maybe she should help them form an attachment. Femili groaned inside. Was she turning into Aunt Norris? "Edwin is very pious. He loves Gaion and wants to serve him."

"So, is he very serious about joining the priesthood and living a life of virginity? There is no way he would ever change his mind?"

"Why?" Femili couldn't help but feel a little uncomfortable with this line of questioning. Though she realized that Meril was a better fit for Edwin, she didn't really want to imagine them ... well, fitting each other.

Meril closed her parasol as the first sun had already set and the second sun was low in the sky. "I just cannot imagine myself with a priest."

Well, do not try too hard, Femili thought.

"It would be such a restrictive life. I need to be free. I like to travel around the galaxy and try new, sometimes shockingly new, things."

"Excuse me for asking, but if you fear Edwin will limit your potential for living your life to its fullest, why even entertain the idea of being with him?"

"He intrigues me," Meril said. "I don't think I have ever been so bewildered by a man. I feel I have to have him. My curiosity will not be satisfied until he is mine."

Well, at least she was honest. It might not have been for the purest of reasons, but at least she was making it clear what her goal was. Femili could somehow respect her intentions even though those intentions were for her cousin and the man she loved. It was an odd and twisted rationalization but no odder and more twisted than her being in love with her cousin. In any case, she respected Meril more than she did Hin'Rik at the moment. He seemed dead set on ruining both Marziah and Ju'Lya for absolutely no reason at all.

"What is that expression?" Meril asked after looking at a silent Femili for a while. "Is there someone else? I don't mind if there is. I can handle competition."

Femili took a deep breath and steadied her emotions. She was actually very good at that for a half human. Her father could rarely control his emotions.

It was probably what drew her mother to him. Not many women, even AiJalonian women, could resist a man passionately declaring his love. In any case, she must have gotten her ability to hide her true feelings from her mother. It was the only explanation for why she didn't immediately burst into tears and declare that Edwin was hers and forever would be. Instead, she said, "There is no one else who can be with him. If you desire him, try to make him yours. But I warn you, Edwin is pure in heart. He will not be with someone he does not love."

"Really?" Meril asked, honestly curious. "This is not the impression I got when he kissed me the first night we were alone."

"He did what?"

***

"You kissed her?" Femili yelled, bursting into Edwin's room that evening. He was too shocked to respond immediately as it was the first time she had ever entered his room unannounced and it was the first time she had said a word to him since their make out session under the waterfall.

"I did," he said once he regained his senses.

Femili let out a Minnithite curse which loosely translated to "I would rather dig my eyes out with a hot fork and then have a feisty dragon spit into the empty sockets than look at you at the moment." Thankfully, Edwin only understood about half of her colorful language. "Why would you do something like that?" she asked.

"Do you want the truth or do you want what I try tell myself?"

"What do you mean? What do you tell yourself?"

"Oh, I tell myself a lot of things," he began as he took a step closer to her. "I tell myself that a kiss means nothing. I tell myself that I can kiss anyone and it will feel exactly the same. I tell myself that I can be like an Engorian and show passion to someone I am not in love with. And even though every time I tell myself these things, it makes me sick to my stomach, I keep trying because the truth is just too hard to bear." With each sentence, he took a step closer to her until finally he was so close he could hear her breathing. "The truth is all my life I have felt nothing. I have been cold, empty and alone. Then the precise moment I looked at you, I went from feeling nothing to feeling everything all at once. What kind of cruel joke of Gaion is this?"

He paused. He went to touch her face then balled his hand into a fist and punched his side instead. "The truth is I love you, Femili. I am in love with you. And I want you so badly that my whole body aches." Edwin took a deep breath and let it out slowly as if he was trying to gain control of himself. "Femili Primme, if you do not leave this room in the next three seconds, I won't be able to let you go tonight."

Femili was momentarily paralyzed. She didn't know what she expected when she confronted Edwin about Meril, but she certainly wasn't expecting this.

"I'm serious, Fem." His voice was shaking. "You need to go."

Instead of leaving immediately, Femili clutched his shirt and rested her head on his chest. "Edwin." Her voice was a plea. A plea for something he couldn't grant.

"Please go."

"What if I don't want to?" she said softly.

"I have said too much. I need you to leave."

Femili nodded. "Okay." Then after taking a deep breath to gather her strength, she turned and left the room.

Chapter 12

Femili realized her mistake. She had no business entering Edwin's room and then demanding to know what he did with his lips. It was none of her concern. She could not let herself get too close to him again. So she preceded to try to blend into the background. If she wasn't in the picture, maybe the feelings they had for one another would no longer grow. Maybe instead, Edwin would form an attachment with Meril. That would be for the best. For a few days, she succeeded in being barely there. But then, Thom returned.

"Oh, hello," Thom said, entering the dining room suddenly. "I wasn't aware that we had visitors."

"Yes, Thom dear." Aunt Norris took the liberty of

answering for everyone. "This is Hin'Rik and Meril Crawly. They are visiting AiJalon from Engor. On vacation for an entire year as it so happens. Oh, and they are brother and sister, not a couple of any sort."

Thom gave his aunt a look that said, "I didn't ask and I don't care."

"What are you doing back so soon?" Marziah asked. "I thought you and Father were attending to some business on Pentauch."

"Something came up that I must attend to. I am only here for a day and then I am off again."

"So soon?" Meril asked. "I was hoping to get to know all the Berzams during our stay here."

"Stay here? At Mansfield Park? Mother, are they staying at Mansfield Park?" Thom asked.

Comtesa Berzam was slightly startled at being addressed in conversation. Once it registered that someone was talking to her, she had to have her son repeat the question before answering. "Well, not that I am aware of. But given that we have so many extra rooms, they are certainly welcome to stay over some time if they like."

"That would be highly inappropriate," Thom said. "Too many single people under one roof would hardly be approved by the Ministry of Purity." Thom excused himself then turned to head upstairs to his room when Ju'Lya noticed something poking out of his bag.

She gasped. "Brother, is that a CSA?" CSA or Cosmo Summit Accoutrement consisted of goggles and sensory gloves. When two people wore then and tuned into the same frequency, they were able to simulate dancing since actual dancing was thought to be too much physical contact within Cosmo city limits. Unfortunately, over the years, young AiJalonians were able to figure out how to circumvent the program to simulate other even more inappropriate behaviors. CSAs had started to get a rather racy and indelicate reputation.

"Why do you have a CSA?" Ju'Lya asked, standing. Within seconds she was rifling through his bag. "He has more than one. He has enough for all of us."

"No, these are not ... " Thom tried to protest, but Ju'Lya had managed to empty his bag and was already handing out CSAs to anyone within arm's reach.

Meril was once again shocked by the Berzam men. The pious and pure Edwin had kissed her on the first night they had met. And now the elder brother Thom had mentioned the Ministry of Purity in one breath and in the next displayed a collection of questionable CSAs. Edwin and Thom were two lessons in contradiction and she needed further study.

"He isn't usually that cross," Femili said, sitting next to Meril.

"What? Who?" she asked.

"Thom. I noticed you looking at him. He comes off very gruff due to his demeanor and his stature, but he is actually rather intuitive and calm."

"Intuitive and calm you say?"

Femili nodded. "He also seems rather tired tonight. He looks as though he hasn't slept for days. I haven't the faintest idea what could be the cause of it."

Meril decided to ponder Thom's character more later. Right now, she needed to take advantage of actually having a CSA in her hands. She had only heard of them before. Of course, on Engor, they were completely unnecessary.

If she wanted to dance with someone, she just did it. No need to simulate it virtually. Same with the other things that the CSA was capable of simulating. Engorians did not believe in withholding the joy of physical pleasures. But she looked forward to using her naivety to her advantage.

"How exactly do you use these?" Hin'Rik asked as he held up his CSA. Damn it, he beat her to it.

"I'll show you, Hin'Rik," Marziah volunteered as her fiancé looked on, confused.

"Shouldn't Ju'Lya demonstrate it for him, dearest?" he asked.

"I am much more familiar with its use than Ju'Lya," Marziah responded. "I have had more occasion to go to Cosmo than my little sister. And shouldn't the most experienced do the teaching? I mean, if I had a question about flickerfish, I could ask no one else but you, wouldn't you agree?"

"Oh, yes, well ... "

"Then it is settled. Hin'Rik, shall we dance?"

It happened so quickly that even Ju'Lya was startled by how she had lost a dance partner. She plopped down next to her mother, probably hoping for reinforcements, but alas, Comtesa Berzam was already asleep.

"What about you, Edwin?" Meril asked. "Would you like to show me how it is done?"

"I don't think that—"

"I have an awful time dealing with rejection," she said, interrupting him. "I guess I will just have to use

Femili."

"Me? What?" Before she knew what was happening, Meril was placing the goggles on Femili's face and slipping the gloves on her hands.

Though Meril had never actually used a CSA before, the control layout was pretty standard and similar to the virtual reality games they had back home. She was even able to create a holographic projection of the two of them dancing.

She wasn't sure if her plan would work, but she thought she could pique Edwin's curiosity enough to have him take over for Femili.

Meril pulled Femili in tighter, virtually of course, but the software was so realistic that Femili was very uncomfortable and tried to twist away.

"Okay," Edwin said. "I will ... I can ... Um ... Femili, give me your goggles and gloves."

Her plan worked. She had attained the desired goal with Edwin joining her on the CSA. But for a moment she wondered about his motivation. Did he take Femili's place because he wanted virtual contact with Meril or was it to protect Femili from any further discomfort? She wasn't sure.

Femili felt very uncomfortable embracing Meril using

the CSA. But watching Edwin with Meril was definitely worse. She tried to avert her eyes and focus on the other side of the room, but there was Marziah and Hin'Rik engaging in some serious heavy breathing. Ju'Lya also noticed the intimacy between the two and made her disapproval known by trying to interrupt every five minutes or so. Mr. Rushworth seemed completely oblivious to the precarious situation that his future wife was engaged in as he read an article about flickerfish on his TelEx.

"Don't you find this worrisome?" Femili asked Mr. Rushworth, hoping that he would intervene.

"Oh, yes, there seems to be a shortage of flickerfish in the Penuel Sea," he said. "The experts seem to think it is due to a foreign bacterium that is elevated this year for some reason."

"No, Mr. Rushworth," Femili said. "What I mean to say is—"

"What is going on here?" Comte Berzam's voice bellowed through the parlor room.

"Father!" Ju'Lya said, standing.

All the CSA participants immediately whipped off their goggles. "Father, we weren't expecting you back so soon," Marziah volunteered, still breathing heavily.

"That does not answer my question. What is going on here?" he asked again. "Edwin, explain."

"Well, you see ... " Edwin was at a loss for words. For there weren't any words that could cleanse this dirty situation. He definitely wouldn't be able to lie about it. A lie wouldn't help any way as Comte Berzam could clearly see that his son and daughter were both cavorting on a CSA with individuals with whom they were not married.

"Thom brought home CSAs," Ju'Lya volunteered. "We were just trying them out."

"Thom? Thom is here?" Comte Berzam asked. "How dare he leave me on Pentauch to come home and play."

It was a genius move on the part of Ju'Lya. The Berzam boys were held to a higher standard than the girls. More was always expected out of Thom and Edwin because they were the oldest and because they were male.

Thom especially had a certain protocol of behavior to follow since he was set to inherit the majority of the estate and most likely the entirety of Comte Berzam's business if and when he decided to retire. Most of the time Thom lived up to his obligations. He was a diligent student of his father. But recently, he had been acting strangely. Disappearing at all hours of the day and night and not just for short periods of time. Sometimes he was gone for days on end without a word. When he would finally return home, he would retreat to his room and request a medical droid. If Femili thought hard, this behavior started shortly after she arrived at Mansfield Park and had steadily increased over the past three years. Apparently, it was getting even worse if Thom was now abandoning his father outright while on business trips.

In any case, shifting the attention to Thom was a brilliant move on the part of Ju'Lya. The Berzam girls could get away with just about anything if they merely focused on the many sins of Thom.

A screaming match ensued between Thom and Comte Berzam upstairs as Ju'Lya tried to keep the party going downstairs.

"It is now my turn on the CSA with Hin'Rik," she said.

Femili had to force herself to not laugh at the foolish desperation dripping from her younger cousin.

"Is something funny, Miss Femili Primme?" Hin'Rik asked.

"Yes, quite. But it is more entertaining when kept to myself."

"How can you be sure about that though? Maybe I

should help you decide by being a fair and honest judge for you."

The smile left Femili's face. "I am really not sure there is an honest bone in your body."

"So you admit it?" Hin'Rik asked slyly.

"Admit what?"

"That you have been thinking about my body." Hin'Rik said this in human English, probably expecting no one else but Femili and maybe his sister to understand. But he didn't realize that Femili had spent the last three years teaching Edwin human English just for fun. They enjoyed being able to talk to each other without having anyone else understand. It was as if they had their own secret code.

"On that note," Edwin said in AiJish, interrupting the banter going on between Femili and Hin'Rik, "why don't we end the evening here?"

"But I didn't get a turn," Ju'Lya whined. "When are we ever going to have this opportunity again? Father will probably confiscate them this evening."

"I believe I am in agreement with Ju'Lya," Meril said. "I find these devices rather diverting."

"Marziah, why don't you see your fiancé home? And Hin'Rik and I will continue," Ju'Lya said. Once again, pretty brilliant move to get Hin'Rik all to herself. Ju'Lya was certainly picking up on a lot of subtle strategies. She must have been learning from the Crawlys.

"Mr. Rushworth can find his own way home," Marziah said.

"All of our visitors will be finding their way home," Edwin said definitively. "This was a bad idea to begin with and I am ending it here. Meril, Hin'Rik, Mr. Rushworth: I will see you another day. Femili, may I see you in the conservatory this instant?"

Femili followed Edwin into the large conservatory of Mansfield Park where Mrs. Norris kept a wide-ranging variety of plants from all over the galaxy. No one was really sure why she insisted on the conservatory being at Mansfield Park instead of her own residence.

But if the Berzams ever noticed their maintenance bill for the upkeep of all the plants, they would realize they were saving Mrs. Norris a small fortune in fees.

"What is going on, Edwin?" Femili asked.

"Why are you flirting with Hin'Rik?"

"Flirting? What are you talking about?"

"The comment about his body. Are you really interested in his body?"

"Gaion, no! What is wrong with you? I have no more interest in Hin'Rik Crawly than I do warts on a grasshopper."

"Are you sure about that?"

"Of course, I'm sure about ... Wait a minute? Why do you even care? I can't believe you even noticed after being so enthralled with your CSA partner."

"I only took over because I was afraid you would be uncomfortable being in intimate proximity with Meril."

"Oh, a fine excuse! Do not think for one second that I haven't noticed how close you have gotten with her!"

"What else am I supposed to do?"

Femili peeked over her shoulder to make sure no one else in the house had heard their yelling.

This was the first time that either of them had ever raised their voices at each other. It was their first fight.

Edwin turned away from her and focused his attention on a Loquay plant from Tentor as he tried to gain his composure. "What do I do, Fem? Just tell me what I am supposed to do so that I no longer feel this way."

"If I knew, I would obey my own counsel first."

Edwin was still staring at the Loquay plant when Femili reached her hand out and brushed it against his. He reacted by grabbing her hand and intertwining their fingers.

"I'm sorry for yelling," he said.

"Me too."

They stayed holding hands and not looking at each other for several moments.

"I don't think it is possible for me to pray this away. I've never prayed more in my life and my feelings aren't going away. They just get stronger. I—"

Femili dropped his hand and instead wrapped her arms around his waist while burying her head in his chest.

"I can't take this anymore," he continued, although he did not push her away. In fact, he pressed her closer to him.

"What's the alternative?" Femili asked.

"Orthodox Miniran."

She knew exactly what he was referring to. It was the strictest order of the priesthood that did not allow marriage or in most cases any contact with the opposite sex. He was going to try to force Gaion to separate them.

Chapter 13

"How did you get away from your father?" Jason Barvery asked as he continued checking his inventory of medical supplies.

Thom sighed. "I just told him I was going drinking on Lumerca. He has such a low opinion of me that he easily believed it."

"Ever consider telling the truth?"

"That was the truth. I stopped on Lumerca, had a drink then came to Oroton 4."

"You know that's not what I mean."

"What? You expect me to tell my father the truth about what I really do when I'm not on AiJalon? That I fly around the galaxy getting into equalizer fights?"

"Come now. That is not the whole truth. You save lives. You have literally saved the lives of hundreds of girls."

"Are any of those girls nobility? Are any of them related to members of the government? I assure you, my father would not care about hundreds of human girls headed for slavery."

"Suit yourself."

"Let me help you," Thom said, lifting a container marked in a language he couldn't read. "What does this say anyway?"

"It says 'Do Not Touch' in Greek so please keep your large, oafish hands off of it." Barvery smacked him on the hands for emphasis.

He obeyed and sat back to watch Barvery work. Thom realized he wasn't the brains of missions like this. Thom was the brawn. He excelled in fighting. After living a lifetime in a repressive household on an even more repressive planet, he rather enjoyed being able to let loose and punch someone's face in.

The repression on AiJalon wasn't even the worst part. He hated living a life of less. A life that was meaningless, pointless, senseless, and useless. He merely existed before he found his purpose with Jason and Mac.

"Can I ask you a question?" Thom asked after a few minutes.

"You just did."

Thom sighed. "Seriously. I have a serious question."

Jason nodded his acceptance.

"What is the probability that a half-human, half-AiJalonian mistura is born with gill flaps?"

Jason Barvery looked up from his TelEx. "Are you asking me because I'm human?"

"What?"

"Because I'm not completely human. My great grandmother was Lumercan."

"No, idiot. I am asking you because you are a doctor and really smart."

"Damn, straight. You know I am the youngest human to ever—"

"Graduate from the Intergalactic Medical Academy," Thom interrupted his friend. "Yes, I know. You've only mentioned it nine hundred and eighty-seven times since I've met you."

"That is completely true. I used to say I was the youngest graduate ever, but then that punk kid from Revua who was only three weeks younger than me, mind you, graduated and took my title."

"You are really going to have to let that go."

"I held the record for six years," Jason said under his breath as he went back to the calculations on his TelEx. "Gill flaps. Human. AiJalonian," he said a few minutes later. "Right. That's a zero percent probability."

"Zero?"

"Yes. It is not possible. Gill flaps are a recessive gene. If a mistura has them, then the human parent must at least be half AiJalonian."

Thom thought about his Uncle Primme. He was definitely fully human. Which begged the question "Who or what exactly was Miss Femili Primme?"

"Why do you ask?" Jason continued without looking up from his work. "Is there a mistura that has caught your eye?"

"Yes, but not in the way you imagine. It is my cousin. Upon visual inspection, she is completely AiJalonian. But my uncle is human."

"Yes, Femili, right? You've mentioned her before." Jason paused and looked at his friend. "She has gill flaps?"

Thom nodded.

"Does it really bother you that much that you are related to a human? Like I said, if she has gill flaps, she's at most one-fourth human. That's not too bad, right?"

"I have nothing against humans. Some of my best friends are humans. Present company included."

"Thanks, man."

"My problem is in the exactitude of language. I do not like calling someone human when they are only half human. And I don't like calling someone half human when they are a quarter human."

"I won't pretend to understand your need for exact language, but I will help you. When you return home, send me a DNA sample. I can let you know in a matter of minutes what she really is."

Thom was silent for so long that Jason thought he had said something wrong.

"This is really bugging you, huh?" Jason asked.

"Yes. And I do not know why," Thom said. "There's something about her that just doesn't ... I don't know ... fit. It's not just the human/AiJalonian thing. It's also how much she knows. I know humans can be smart. I mean, look at you. You are the smartest person perhaps in the galaxy."

"Once again, thanks, man."

"She knows things she shouldn't know. Remember that time I took Mac in my brother's guster to Capernica?"

"Yeah, I had to drug you so you could lie about your whereabouts."

"Well, she figured out where I was and how and why I was lying. How could someone who has never left Minnith know things like that?"

"And you've been letting these questions sit in your brain for years? Why didn't you ask me earlier?"

He shrugged. "I like her. She's more than a cousin. She's like a sister to me. I think a part of me doesn't want to know the truth."

Jason sighed and went over to his control panel. He knew his friend had amazingly good instincts. It became a side effect of the dangerous lives they lived. If Thom felt something was off with his half-human cousin, he was probably right. "Look, if you know the Simulating Ingression Code to the medical droid in your house, I should be able to access it remotely. Then your cousin would just need to put in a sample. I could give you an answer immediately."

"Sim what now?" To Thom, it was like Jason was speaking that Greek language he had just seen.

"God! And you are supposed to be the superior species? Dude, I can't help you if you don't know the SIC number. You're going to have to wait."

Thom aimlessly wandered around the cargo bay trying not to get in the way while figuring out a nonsuspicious way to ask his next question.

"So where is Mac hiding?" he asked, hoping he wasn't being obvious in his intentions.

"You know Mac. Just partying on Lumerca proper. There is a lot more trouble to get into down there than on a boring moon like Oroton 4. But she also made good use of the CSAs you brought. She was able to get the required intel for our next mission."

"Hmm," Thom said, trying to figure out an excuse to go back down to Lumerca.

Jason paused his work and looked at his friend again. "You are trying to think of a reason to go back down to the planet and find Mac, aren't you?"

"I am not," Thom said defiantly.

Jason rolled his eyes. A very human thing to do. "Your lips are swelling."

"What? No, they are not." Thom touched his lips. They were definitely swelling.

"Yes, they are. Which means you're lying. You AiJalonians are so easy to read. Please never play a game of poker against a human. You will most definitely lose."

"Poker? What is a game of poker?"

"In any case," Jason said, ignoring the question, "Mac isn't here. And if you like my little sister so much please just tell her."

Did Thom really like Mac? Who was he kidding? He really did.

For a long time, he had just been curious about her. When he met the two of them on that fateful night three years ago, he never would have guessed they were even related, let alone brother and sister. Jason was a poor, oddly smart human and she was a filthy rich yet mischievous Lumercan. And they even had completely different surnames. Mac Clintok and Jason Barvery. After knowing them for a little while, it got even more unclear. It turned out that Mac was half human and half Lumercan, which could mean they had the same human mother and different fathers, right? Wrong?

Mac's mother was Lumercan and her father was human. So did they have the same father and just chose to take the surnames of their mothers? No, that was wrong as well.

Finally, Thom just gave up on trying to figure out their family genealogy and just asked. But that didn't clear up matters too much either.

It turned out that they were really aunt and nephew because Mac's older half-sister was Jason's mother. But they were raised as brother and sister by Mac's mother, not on Lumerca (which would make sense) but on AiJalon. It took months for Thom to figure all this out. He was obsessed with it for a while until he finally figured out that he wasn't really obsessed with Mac's family tree. He was really just obsessed with Mac herself.

Is that what was happening with his obsession with Femili's DNA? Was he subconsciously attracted to her? He shook his head. That wasn't it. There was something definitely peculiar going on with her origin story and he was going to figure it out.

"Why are you shaking your head?" he heard a voice say behind him. Thom turned around to see Mac standing there in the flesh. Gaion, she was beautiful. He didn't know if he was more attracted to her human genetics or her Lumercan genetics or maybe it was the mix. In any case, she was the perfect embodiment of feminine strength. She looked just as beautiful in an expensive Lumercan ball gown as she did in her current attire of spandex pants strapped with weapons.

Either way she glowed. Literally. All Lumercans did. Their glow was a unique phenotype developed to attract a mate and Thom was attracted to Mac like a moth to a flame.

"Nothing. I wasn't—"

"Careful," she said with a smile. "Your lips will swell. It's your tell."

"Told you," Jason chimed in.

"Don't worry. It makes your lips even sexier," she said. Mac Clintok giggled to herself as she took her equalizer out of its holster and checked the settings.

"Gross, please stop," Jason said.

Thom didn't know how to react. Was she just kidding? Was she just flirting? Did she really find him sexy? Would she agree to a mutual flirtation if he asked for one? How could one woman make him doubt everything all at once?

Mac and Jason started arguing in a foreign language that Thom didn't understand. He suddenly regretted not being more studious. Most AiJalonians spoke dozens of languages. They were supposed to be one of the most intelligent species.

Even if he didn't exactly understand the language, he knew they were most likely having the same fight they always did. Jason would be claiming that because he was older, he was in charge and she needed to listen to him and Mac would be saying that age didn't matter because she was the aunt and he was the nephew and he had to listen to her. Next a physical struggle would ensue in which Mac would quickly assume dominance by putting Jason into a headlock until he cried auntie.

Chapter 14

"Is Miss Femili Primme out in society?" Hin'Rik asked suddenly during lunch a week after Thom had left with the mildly entertaining CSAs.

Femili was starting to wonder if Hin'Rik and Meril had moved into Mansfield Park unbeknownst to her. They were there so often she saw them more than she saw Thom.

Mrs. Norris almost choked on her soup. "Why would you ask such a question?"

"I am rather curious," he said. "She is eighteen and unmarried. If her younger cousin Ju'Lya is out in society, why is she not?"

"Well, that is actually a good question," Comtesa

Berzam said. "I don't think we have ever thought about it. Femili, would you like to present to society?"

Femili continued refilling the drink glasses as she said, "Is it necessary?"

"Only if you ever want to get married," Meril said. "How are eligible men supposed to meet you if you never attend summits?"

"I believe Femili is correct in this matter," Mrs. Norris said. "Having a summit in Femili's name is completely unnecessary. She is a human. What respectable AiJalonian would marry her?"

"Aunt," Edwin said, "that is unkind."

"That is the truth," she said. "Also, she is a servant."

Hin'Rik smiled. "Unless I am mistaken, there is no such thing as a living servant on AiJalon."

"That is actually true," Comtesa Berzam said. "And since she is not legally a servant, and is still a half-AiJalonian woman, I believe it is past due for her summit."

"Must we?" Femili said.

"What is the matter, Femili?" Hin'Rik asked. "Are you afraid of being too dashing?"

"Do not tease her, brother," Meril said. "We all know that Femili despises attention as much as you crave it."

"It is not that I despise attention," Femili said. "Attention that is warranted is welcome. I just don't see the need for a party in my name just because I have turned eighteen. If it is so that I can bring myself to the attention of eligible bachelors, I can assure you there is no need. I am fully aware of the type of man I desire and it is not one that needs to have women displayed at a dance like a feast ready to be consumed."

Hin'Rik had to stifle a laugh.

"Oh, Femili, do not deny us the opportunity for a party. We so rarely have the chance to celebrate," Comtesa Berzam said.

Femili sighed. Though most people thought her Aunt Berzam was an annoyance who only slept and drank, Femili had actually gotten quite close to her. She didn't ask for much besides Femili's companionship and she wanted to thank her for all the care she had given her over the years. How could she reject such a simple request?

"We can have a summit," she said quietly.

"What was that?" Hin'Rik said, though everyone knew that he heard her. He obviously enjoyed teasing her.

Hin'Rik had several ulterior motives for inquiring about a summit for Femili.

First, sitting around Mansfield Park was still proving to be boring even with the game he had going with his sister. Second, dancing was not only great entertainment, but it was an excellent excuse to come in close contact with pretty girls. And finally, he just wanted to see Femili dressed up. He knew she would be exquisite. And with the beauty of Femili on display, it would send both Marziah and Ju'Lya into hissy fits of desperation.

Truth be told, Femili was slightly excited for a summit in her honor. She didn't show it, but really, what woman wouldn't be excited at the prospect of dressing up and commanding the attention of the room? But she was also extremely nervous. She really didn't have any appropriate clothing. The only thing remotely fancy that she owned was the monochromatic clothing unit that Madam Noonan had let her borrow three years ago. While that would have been completely appropriate and even formal in Cosmo, out here on the islands it would have been considered bland. She knew her cousins Marziah and Ju'Lya would never let her borrow anything. She wasn't sure what to do.

She looked at the MCU again. She wouldn't even be able to wear it if she wanted to as she had outgrown it. But she did recall that Madam Noonan told her to call if she ever needed anything. Did this count? She decided to give it a try.

Marziah and Ju'Lya had no intention of helping their cousin prepare for her event. They were mutually miserable at just the idea of Femili getting more attention than them. They hoped with all their hearts that she would have nothing to wear and would be completely embarrassed by showing up in just one of her daily dressing gowns.

Even Edwin was concerned about what she would wear. But he had no clue how to help the situation. He thought about asking her what she needed and then going to buy it for her. But would that be appropriate? While he deliberated back and forth on what to do, time got the better of him and the day of the summit appeared.

Chapter 15

Hin'Rik Crawly realized his miscalculation the moment he saw Femili Primme descend the grand staircase into the ballroom of Mansfield Park. He had taken it upon himself to invite every single AiJalonian there was in the nearest three archipelagos to the summit announcing Femili's eligibility. He had even instructed them to pay special attention to Femili. Hin'Rik accurately predicted that the inordinate amount of attention on Femili would cause both Marziah and Ju'Lya to melt like butter in his hand. But he inaccurately predicted his own feelings toward the sight of Femili.

He knew she was attractive; he knew she was intriguing; but until he saw her dressed in formal island wear, he had no idea that she was absolutely mesmerizing.

There was no need to instruct any of the perspective suitors to pay special attention to her. At this point, he would have to pay men to ignore her so that he could get a moment alone with her. And suddenly, that was all he wanted. Just one moment in her presence.

Edwin was strangely comforted to see how much attention Femili commanded. It was reassuring to see that his attraction to her was not unwarranted. It was not irrational to believe she was beautiful even though she was half human. He wouldn't have cared if it was though. Even if he was the only one in the galaxy to believe she was lovely he was completely fine with it. He also delighted in the knowledge that she would not be alone. There would be someone out there who would earn the privilege to marry her. Someone who would take care of her. No one would be worthy of her, but if tonight was any indication, there were plenty out there willing to try.

"Are you in awe of your cousin?" Meril asked as the evening progressed.

"Yes," Edwin answered without thinking. He then

cleared his throat and attempted to offer a truthful, yet not incestuous explanation. "She certainly looks the part of a prestigious AiJalonian woman. She will—" Edwin paused and took a deep breath before continuing. "She will marry well and bring honor and status to our family."

"Indeed," Meril agreed. "And what about you? Have you any thoughts to your own marriage?" Meril wasn't quite sure why she asked such a thing. Did she really care whether he intended on marrying or not? Wasn't this all just a game? She had already gotten a tremendous amount of points from Edwin on their first encounter, but given that he was the only male Berzam around, he was her only hope to defeat Hin'Rik and he hadn't so much as held her hand since their first kiss. She had to take things further. Meril wondered where his erogenous zones were. For AiJalonians, it was usually their gill flaps. She reached out to caress his when suddenly Ju'Lya approached.

"Where did she get that gown, Edwin?" she asked.

Meril lowered her hand and sighed. This petty child was getting in the way of her progress.

Edwin merely shrugged, not wanting to engage his sister in a debate about his cousin.

"I bet she stole it," Ju'Lya continued. "It looks really

expensive and humans are known to steal things."

"And just when exactly would she have had time to steal it?" Edwin said as he stared at the sixth single AiJalonian asking Femili to dance. It had actually been nine dances but only six men. Several were on their second dance. Edwin felt sick to his stomach. He finished the wine in his glass before saying, "The summit was announced two days ago and she hasn't left the house since. Stop being illogical, Ju'Lya."

Ju'Lya responded with something whiny and petulant but honestly, he wasn't listening anymore. Instead, he watched as Femili declined the offer to dance and instead headed out of the ballroom. Where was she going? Was she tired? Did she need a drink? Maybe he should follow her. But why? What would he do once he caught up to her? It didn't matter. He needed to talk to her.

Edwin grabbed another glass of wine from a passing droid and headed in her direction.

***

"And just where are you running off to, Miss Femili Primme?" Hin'Rik Crawly asked her before she could make a clean escape from the ballroom.

Femili paused her retreat and turned to him. "I am

under no obligation to tell you anything."

He smiled. It was annoying how good-looking he was when he smiled. "Well, I feel as if I am under obligation to tell you that you are completely stunning this evening."

"Let me relieve you of that obligation. I neither need nor desire your validation of my appearance. In the future, you may keep those comments to yourself."

"You continue to surprise me, Miss Femili Primme. How is it you keep me wondering about you?"

"Trust me, it is unintentional," she said. "Perhaps the thought of my relieving myself will rid you of this side effect of my presence." With that she swept past him and into the bathroom.

When she exited, Edwin was waiting for her. "Are you all right?" he asked.

"Yes, why?"

"I thought you might have taken ill. You have had four glasses of sweet punch this evening. I know such sweet drinks do not sit well in your stomach. I was worried."

Her heart smiled. "Thank you for worrying about me."

They stared at each other for a moment before Edwin said, "May I dance with you?"

"Do you really think that is a good idea for us?"

"No," he said honestly. "It doesn't mean I don't want to."

"There are a lot of things we want that cannot be. I think we should accept them."

Edwin took a deep breath and let her walk past him.

"So, where were we?" Meril said when he returned to his place by her side. "Ah, yes, I believe we were talking about your future plans for marriage." She reached her hands toward his gill flaps.

"Don't touch me there. It doesn't work on me," he said before she reached her goal. He grabbed another glass of wine and finished it in one gulp. "I will not be getting married. I am joining the Orthodox Miniran Order."

Chapter 16

Hin'Rik Crawly had not been able to rid Femili from his mind no matter how much he flirted and cavorted with other women. He tried not to watch Femili too closely during the summit and had willed himself to only dance with her once, but his will was slowly breaking. The next day, with his sweet words and charm, he was able to convince Ju'Lya to meet him secretly after the second sunset. In truth, he was just hoping to catch a glimpse of Femili.

The gods of passion must have been smiling down on him.

When he arrived at the designated meeting location, he found Femili, not Ju'Lya. Had she found out about the planned, clandestine rendezvous and was now trying to intercept?

Was she beginning to feel toward him the desire that was growing in himself? Or was this merely a coincidence and he was seriously overthinking things? He had to feel this situation out.

"Miss Primme, how are you this lovely evening?"

Femili looked at him as if he were a sea monster from Tentor. "What are you doing here, Mr. Crawly?"

Well, that was a clear sign that it was merely a coincidence. He looked around a little to see if Ju'Lya was on her way.

"Are you expecting someone?" Femili asked.

"Maybe I am expecting you," he said, turning on the charm.

"No. No, no, no. Don't try that with me." She wagged her finger in the air as if she were admonishing a schoolchild.

"Try what?"

"The insincere compliments, the secret caresses, the forced charm. I am not Ju'Lya. I am not Marziah. Your empty, Engorian platitudes will not work on me."

Hin'Rik was taken aback but not defeated. He had yet to meet a woman he couldn't woo. He certainly was not going to let little Femili Primme be the first. "I feel as though

I should be offended, but honestly any words from your lips are just too sweet to me."

Femili stared at him with an exasperated expression. "I am so happy that I didn't just eat. Else that really would have made me vomit."

"Whoa, that was vicious."

"Aw, I thought all my words were just so sweet to you." She chuckled. "You are ridiculous. I can scarcely be angry with you because you are just that laughable."

"You really do not like me, do you?"

"You mistake me, sir. Disliking you would be far more effort for you than I am willing to give."

Hin'Rik touched his chest and feigned pain. "I must admit, that stung a little. You have a way with words, Miss Femili Primme."

She took a deep breath. "Whatever. Close your eyes."

"What?"

"I said close your eyes, Mr. Crawly. Should I say it in an Engorian language? I know three." Just for emphasis, Femili repeated the command in the three languages she knew to be popular on Engor.

"Okay, I understand. I am closing my eyes."

While his eyes were closed, she ran behind a tree and

then whipped off her dressing gown to reveal her bodysuit. "I'm going for a swim," she called as she ran toward the water. "Enjoy your little secret rendezvous with ... You know, I don't even care. Goodbye." With that she jumped into the lake, leaving Hin'Rik alone, shocked, and speechless. He smiled. Then he laughed. Femili Primme was not at all what he expected. And he liked it. A lot.

He stayed and watched over the lake as she swam back and forth. At some point Ju'Lya showed up, but she barely registered in his peripheral. Moments later, she left as she was not getting the attention she desired from Hin'Rik.

Femili swam for hours. Hin'Rik just stayed and watched. After a while, he started to get genuinely concerned for her. Why on AiJalon was she swimming alone in a lake in the middle of the night? It was almost as if she was running from something, but given that the lake was a confined space, her running away just transformed into a monotonous back and forth.

Finally, a few minutes before the first sunrise, she came to the edge of the lake. He could see that the hours of swimming had taken a toll on her body. Her legs wobbled beneath her. Hin'Rik took off his coat and wrapped it around her as he steadied her on her feet. Thankfully, she didn't have the energy to fight him away.

He helped her to the platform where she sat down and then called a droid with the remote embedded in her wristband. Femili breathed heavily as she waited for the drink she had ordered from the servant droid. After she took a few sips, she was finally able to speak.

"Why are you still here?"

"I think the better question is what was that?" He pointed to the lake for emphasis. "Why did you just swim yourself to the point of exhaustion? What are you trying to do?"

Instead of answering, she drank more water.

"Miss Femili Primme, the one who has a way with words. Have you suddenly lost your way?"

Femili still didn't answer.

"Well, I'll just guess. I am rather good at games. Let's see. You are trying to avoid someone or something."

No response.

"It is something that scares you. Something that is scarier than drowning alone in a lake in the middle of the night."

No response.

"Is it an unrequited love perhaps?"

Femili choked on her water.

Hin'Rik patted her on the back as he said, "If I am in error, you really should correct me before I come up with some very interesting scenarios."

"It's the third."

Hin'Rik thought for a moment. He could not figure out to what she was referring. "The third what?"

"On the evening of the third day of the month, I have uncontrollable night terrors. So I do anything to not sleep."

Hin'Rik suddenly felt guilty for teasing her so. He wrapped an arm around her and shockingly she didn't shrug him off. Instead, she leaned onto him. He felt his pulse accelerate. Had her opinion of him changed that quickly? Was she being pulled in by his charm? He looked down and realized he was wrong on both counts. She had fallen asleep.

His heart felt strange in his chest as he looked down on the sleeping Femili on his shoulder. It started to beat irregularly. "What is this?" he asked himself as he literally beat his chest a couple of times to get it to behave properly. It wouldn't obey.

When it became apparent that Femili was not going to wake up anytime soon, Hin'Rik gathered her in his arms and began the trek back to Mansfield.

"What are you doing?" Edwin asked, blocking Hin'Rik's path.

Hin'Rik looked down at Femili and then to Edwin. "I think it is quite obvious. I'm taking her to bed." Hin'Rik smiled.

Edwin could not help himself from becoming enraged at the Engorian's use of the euphemism for sex. He was so angry, he found it impossible to speak for a moment.

"I think an even more interesting question is why are *you* here?"

"What do you mean? I live here."

"You live at Mansfield Park. And at this hour of the morning, you should still be sound asleep in your warm bed in Mansfield Park. Who are you looking for out here?"

"This lake is on our property. I am well within my rights to explore it at any hour of the day." While that was true so Edwin was able to say it without vomiting, the full truth was not as innocent. The full truth was that it was the third of the month and he didn't want Femili to be alone. It was the first third of the month since they had kissed, so he didn't want the temptation of being alone in close contact with her, but he also wanted to make sure she was okay. He wanted to be there in case she fell asleep and woke up terrified. He secretly wanted to be there to hold her in his arms and comfort her. So, seeing her cradled in another man's arms was killing him inside.

"Typical AiJalonian. Talking about your rights when I just asked a simple question. A question that you don't seem to want to answer."

"I will take her from here," Edwin said, reaching to take Femili from Hin'Rik's arms.

Hin'Rik held her closer. "The lady began the evening with me and I will make sure she ends it with me."

Edwin wanted to protest further, but it would be inappropriate. Instead, he watched as Hin'Rik carried her to Mansfield Park. In his mind, he imagined how Hin'Rik would probably gently lay Femili on the bed. From where he stood, watching their figures fade in the distance, Edwin felt powerless, knowing there was nothing he could do.

Chapter 17

After placing Femili in her bed, he stayed for a few moments and watched her sleep. If what she said was true about her night terrors, he wanted to be there for her in case she needed him. It was the first time he could ever remember having this feeling. A completely unselfish feeling where he cared more about what someone else was feeling or might feel than he cared about his own feelings.

Suddenly, the game with his sister wasn't important anymore. It didn't matter that he had already kissed the engaged Marziah and could basically kiss Ju'Lya any time he wanted. He was definitely winning against Meril even though she had kissed Edwin as well.

But none of that mattered. He didn't care. In that moment, all he cared about was another game. The game for Femili's heart. He had to win her heart. Suddenly, there was nothing he wanted more than for her to love him. Nothing else mattered. He knew what he had to do.

When he was sure she wouldn't be waking up, he bounded down the stairs to where the family was eating breakfast. All heads turned toward him as they all wondered why he was in their house so early in the morning and why he was coming from upstairs. Immediately, Mrs. Norris eyed Ju'Lya, but the latter gave a shrug, indicating that she didn't know why he was there either.

"I know you are wondering why I am here at this hour," Hin'Rik began. "And perhaps why I am coming from upstairs. Specifically, from Femili's bedroom."

Ju'Lya and Mrs. Norris gasped.

"It is not what you think, though I wish it were," he said with a wanting sigh.

"Hin'Rik?" Ju'Lya said once her coughing fit subsided. She was so shocked that she choked on her tea.

"I am interested in Miss Femili Primme," Hin'Rik announced. "I would like to officially enter into a mutual flirtation with her or whatever it is you call it on this planet."

"With ... Why ... " Mrs. Norris stuttered. "Excuse me for asking, Mr. Crawly, but have you had drink this early in the morning?"

Hin'Rik smiled. "I'll be back when she is awake to ask her formally."

Edwin lingered at the lake that morning, contemplating his feelings and what he should do. There really was no point in even considering the situation further, but he tried. He was in love with his cousin. He could freely admit it now, to himself at least, but it didn't mean that it was any easier to accept. He took the time alone at the lake to pray and supplicate to Gaion for guidance. How could he go on with a normal life? After he had poured out his heart to the higher being, he returned to Mansfield Park only to learn the most disturbing news. Hin'Rik Crawly wanted to enter into a mutual flirtation with Femili. With *his* Femili. No, she wasn't his. She couldn't be his. But still it felt like a betrayal.

Mrs. Norris didn't wait long to confront Femili about this new development. As soon as Hin'Rik had left Mansfield Park, she practically flew upstairs and flung open the door to her niece's room.

"What did you do?" she yelled venomously.

Femili struggled to pry her eyes open and pull herself away from the brink of exhaustion. "Can you be more specific please? Do you mean what did I do today? Yesterday? Or is this more of a theoretical question?"

"Hin'Rik Crawly!" Mrs. Norris yelled by way of clarification. It did not serve as clarification for Femili. She still had no clue as to what her aunt was referring. But then she looked down at her still damp bodysuit. She recalled some of the events of the evening before. She had seen Hin'Rik at the lake right before her marathon swimming session. Then she had seen him that morning when she finished. How did she get back to her room? Oh no, had he carried her? Did her aunt see?

"I can assure you, aunt. There is nothing between Mr. Crawly and myself. You are free to marry him off to Ju'Lya. There is nothing between us."

"Well, someone should inform him of this."

"What?"

"He just formally asked to enter into a mutual flirtation with you."

Femili was silent for a moment as her aunt's words

replayed in her mind a few times. Was her AiJish that poor? Was she really misunderstanding her aunt so entirely?

"I'm sorry, could you say that again?" Femili asked finally.

"Hin'Rik Crawly wants to enter into a mutual flirtation with you." Aunt Norris was so furious at the situation and the fact that she even had to repeat it that she spat out the words as if they were poison.

So Femili hadn't misheard. In that case, it was obviously a joke on the part of Hin'Rik. Clearly, some Engorian humor that her aunt wasn't picking up on. Femili laughed hysterically. "He was kidding, aunt," she said. "I can assure you he has no intention to enter a serious flirtation with me."

Aunt Norris sighed in relief. "And can you guarantee that you will not enter into an official flirtation with him?"

"Absolutely. My hand to Gaion, I want nothing to do with that expert flirt."

"That is a relief." For the first time since hearing Hin'Rik declare his intention for Femili Mrs. Norris could breathe. All was not lost. She wasn't sure why Hin'Rik found something like this funny, but she was also not Engorian.

She may never understand. But if it was just a joke and he wasn't serious, then there was still hope for Ju'Lya.

Her success as an aunt and matchmaker would be unmatched after attaching both her nieces to such well-off and eligible men. She would be the talk of Queli.

"Honestly, I despise him. Ju'Lya can have him. And make sure she keeps him out of my presence for all eternity."

It didn't take long for every member of the Berzam family to find out Hin'Rik's intentions. Before she knew it, Femili was on a holocall with her uncle Comte Berzam.

"Is it true?" he asked without so much as a hello.

"Is what true?"

"Hin'Rik Crawly. I must say, I did not know you were so capable in catching a suitable mate."

Femili wanted to interrupt and inquire as to just what was so suitable about him, but she decided to remain silent.

"I mean, you are quite attractive for a human, but I didn't realize that you were so attractive as to find such a rich prospect despite your genetics. For I have investigated the Crawly family and found that they are quite prestigious on their home planet. I would have been perfectly happy if he had made an offer to my Ju'Lya. But even with you marrying him it would be quite advantageous and a great alliance between planets and families."

Marriage? He was talking about marriage already and she hadn't even agreed to the flirtation. This was getting insane. Femili began to try to think of a polite way to say that there was no way in hell this attachment was going to happen.

"Uncle, I am quite sure that Hin'Rik was joking and that he actually has no interest in me."

"Do not underestimate yourself as I did. You obviously have some worthwhile qualities."

Her uncle did not even realize how much he had just insulted her. Did he really believe that she was only worthwhile because she had attracted the likes of Hin'Rik Crawly?

"You mistake me, uncle. I am well aware of the qualities I possess. I am also not under the delusion that Hin'Rik Crawly would ever be able to identify, let alone appreciate, those qualities."

***

"What exactly is going on?" Meril asked her brother when he arrived home that morning.

"What do you mean? Nothing out of the ordinary as

far as I know."

"Then why did I just get a hysterical TelEx from Ju'Lya claiming that you are professing your love for Femili?"

"Ah, that." Hin'Rik nodded. "That sounds about right."

"What are you doing? She was not a part of the game."

"And why was she not included?" Hin'Rik asked as he removed his damp shirt.

Meril thought for a moment. She wasn't quite sure why they never included Femili in the game. It could have been because Hin'Rik already had a two to one advantage and didn't need another game piece. Or it could have been because from the moment they met her they both knew she was too smart to play their game.

"Let's not include her. Aren't you having enough fun with Marziah and Ju'Lya?"

"First, those two have begun to bore me. Second—" He paused. "Maybe this isn't a game."

"I do not know if I can believe that."

"Honestly, I am not sure if I believe it yet either," he said with a smile. A flush of warmth overtook him. This was definitely a different feeling and ... he liked it. He liked this feeling a lot. He liked even the idea of being in love with Femili Primme.

"I rather like Femili," Meril said, crossing her arms. She was the first person on AiJalon Meril had encountered that she felt was an intellectual equal. Meril didn't usually care about other's feelings and emotions, but in just a short period of time, she had made a connection with Femili Primme. "How about you try not to destroy her like that girl on Capernica?"

**

Femili thought that would be the end of the absurd talk about her and Hin'Rik, but the day proceeded to unravel further absurdities. As promised, Hin'Rik returned to make a formal request for a mutual flirtation.

The utterly embarrassing moment happened in the parlor in front of the entire Berzam clan. Hin'Rik arrived holding a dozen roses. A flower extremely difficult to find on AiJalon. He had to have spent a fortune on them. But seeing as Femili was half human, Hin'Rik felt it absolutely necessary to present her with what he thought was the perennial symbol of affection for humans.

He presented her with the flowers then said, "You can be under no surprise as to the reason for my visit."

Femili shook her head. "Perhaps you want to show off your prowess in botany?" she said, inspecting the flowers. "Seriously, where on AiJalon did you find earthling roses?"

Hin'Rik smiled. Why did he always seem so amused with her insults? What did she have to do to make it clear that she was not interested in him in any way, shape, or form?

"Your sharp tongue is indeed beguiling."

"Please do not talk about parts of my body. Ever."

"Agreed. Some things cannot be adequately put into words anyway." He leered at her with a wanting smirk.

"And with that, I'm leaving," she said, headed for the door.

"And I'm following."

"Please go away," Femili added once they were outside.

"I cannot do that. See, I was admittedly pampered as a child. I am used to getting what I want." She was a few steps ahead of him and walking briskly to increase that distance. Hin'Rik reached out, grabbed her hand and pulled her to him. "Right now, I want you."

There were so many things wrong with what he had just said she didn't know where to begin. First of all, it just flat out didn't feel the same as when Edwin had told her he wanted her. Second, he just admitted he wanted her for the for now.

"That's the problem, Hin'Rik. You want me right now. Yesterday you wanted Ju'Lya. And the day before that it was Marziah. Who is to say what you will want tomorrow? Perhaps you will find medical droids suddenly sexy. I dare not venture a guess."

"Is that all it is? You doubt my sincerity?" Hin'Rik paused. Honestly, he doubted his own sincerity. How could he blame her for doubting as well? "I understand. You have every reason to. But don't you have to give me a chance to prove it to you? Don't you have to let me show you I'm sincere?"

Femili looked at him incredulously. "You are rather mistaken. I don't have to do anything. I don't owe you a single thing. You are nothing to me."

Her sharp tongue this time was a little less beguiling and a little more cutting.

Chapter 18

Seeing Femili in Hin'Rik's arms broke him inside. Edwin was just a shell. He had lost her. But on the other hand, how could he lose something that was never his? Did he really think he could perhaps marry his own cousin? Not on any planet he could think of. Any two people seeking marriage had to submit to genetic testing. Their family relation would immediately be made known and their marriage would be illegal. They could be prosecuted just for attempting it. If he wanted to be with Femili, they would have to live on some socially backward moon, or worse, in a paedor.

Hin'Rik Crawly. What an appropriate name for Edwin's skin crawled just at the sight of him. What in the world did she see in that double-tongued, hopeless flirt? Did Femili really like him? Was she just desperate for love and affection? Or maybe she was purposely trying to anger Edwin. Yes, that had to be it. She was trying to get his attention by entering into a flirtation with the most infuriating person possible. Well, it worked. She had his attention. And he could play this game as well.

"You are a man deeply troubled," a voice said from behind. Edwin turned to see Meril Crawly approaching him.

He bowed politely then continued to stare out over the lake. He should have been thinking of ways to make conversation with Meril Crawly. If he could learn to flirt with her, especially in front of Femili, it might make her jealous. And then she would see how it felt. He sighed audibly. Then she would know the same kind of pain that he was currently feeling. Was that what he wanted? No. He never wanted her to feel pain.

"That was quite a sigh," Meril said. Edwin had honestly forgotten she was still there. "That was a sigh that can only be expressed by a troubled heart. Am I right?"

He nodded. She was right. Though he hoped she didn't ask any specific questions about the situation.

"Would you like to discuss it with me?"

"No," he answered. That question was easy enough to answer honestly.

"Well, then, we will play a little game. Let us see how well I can surmise what the issue is."

She paused as she stared at Edwin. He relaxed a little. There was no way she would possibly guess that he had an ill-fated love for his fleshly cousin. "It is an unexpressed love," she said a few moments later.

Edwin looked at her, shocked. "I see that I am correct. Even though they rarely have deep emotions, AiJalonians are unable to conceal them."

Edwin was under the mistaken impression that Meril was referring to his unexpressed love with Femili. He had momentarily forgotten that just a few days ago he had willingly kissed Meril and so she was under the impression that she was the target of his love.

"In my mother tongue, we have a word, *fristinlung*," she said. "It describes an overwhelming physical and emotional attraction to someone based solely on your first encounter with them before words are spoken."

Edwin felt his heartbeat accelerate as he thought about the first time he saw Femili at the cargo ship station. It was definitely the *fristinlung* feeling that Meril was describing.

Why did it have to be Femili?

"You don't have to be ashamed of it," Meril continued. "Sometimes our bodies recognize something before our minds do. It is really not something you need to be ashamed of."

"This is not the AiJalonian way," Edwin said. "Attraction, love—these emotions are irrelevant."

"The AiJalonian way is not the only way." Edwin hadn't noticed how close Meril had gotten to him. When he turned his head, her face was inches from his. Before he knew what was happening, she leaned in for a kiss. He had to admit, part of him was relieved that Meril didn't know the truth about his feelings for Femili and thought that his feelings were for her. Another part of him wanted to keep the kiss going in hopes that Femili would catch them and she would feel this pain. But yet another part of him regretted even thinking that and wanted to end the kiss immediately. That part won.

"We shouldn't do this," Edwin said.

"You're right," she said. "We should find a more secluded location."

He sighed. Frustration vibrated every cell in his body. He was frustrated he couldn't be with the one he loved. He was frustrated that Meril kept showing up and misunderstanding him. And he was frustrated that there was nothing he could do to fix either of these situations. "Do you not remember that I am to be a priest?"

"I recall," she said reaching to caress his check. "I am hoping for the opportunity to change your mind.

Edwin grabbed her hand pulled it away from his face. He could see the confusion on her face. He didn't have the energy to clarify. "I'm leaving. Please don't follow."

***

Things had progressed rapidly with Hin'Rik and not in a way that Marziah approved. She'd momentarily had Hin'Rik in her clutches. Finally, a man who was cultured, well-spoken, interesting, and—dare she say it?—who exuded sexual energy. She actually craved his touch, a stark contrast to how she felt around her soon-to-be-husband. Marziah was actually repulsed by the chunky, sweaty hands of her fiancé. Oh, Gaion! Why had she not waited just a few more weeks before she agreed to this unsavory marriage? Then she could have met Hin'Rik and had him all to herself.

Instead, he was hamstrung by her impending marriage. That had to explain why he didn't suggest to her that she break her engagement and marry him instead. After the night of passion they had shared, that was the only possible explanation, right? He wanted to be with her but couldn't. That would also explain why he soon turned his attention to her younger sister. Ju'Lya was merely a replacement for Marziah. They looked alike, though Marziah knew herself to be the more attractive one. But for poor, lovesick Mr. Crawly, it would have to do.

That was what Marziah told herself in order to not feel completely miserable when Hin'Rik began to show her less and less attention. But this explanation did not suffice when Hin'Rik began proclaiming his love for Femili. That was completely and utterly inexplicable. He couldn't possibly really love the half human; he was trying to get Marziah's attention again. Yes, that had to be it. It was a cry for help. With this new logic in mind, she decided to approach Mr. Crawly.

He had gotten into the habit of arriving every day to Mansfield Park with a different bunch of earthlike flowers for Femili.

Obviously, a desperate attempt to make Marziah jealous. She would assuage his hurt feelings and his lovesickness for her. After sending Femili away on some errand to her Aunt Norris, Marziah waited for his arrival.

She expected to see elation on his face when he noticed that they were alone; instead he kept looking around for Femili.

"I don't know what kind of game you are playing, Hin'Rik, but it isn't funny," she said petulantly after she tried to hug him and he removed her arms.

"I am not playing this time," he said calmly. "I think for the first time in my life, I am truly sincere."

Marziah was aghast. "Are you saying I was a game to you?"

Hin'Rik smiled. "Beautiful Marziah," he said, caressing her cheek. "Yes," he said bluntly and then stepped around her in search of Femili.

Did he just say 'yes'? she thought. *I was really a game. But he caressed my cheek so lovingly. How dare he toy with my emotions? I will be no man's toy.*

Marziah was married on the eighth of Swalong. It was a weekday as she was too impatient to wait for the weekend given that she had all the necessary preparations ready for an immediate marriage: a hatred of home, a miserably disappointing flirtation with one man and a general disdain for the man she was to marry. Still the bride was quite beautiful and her bridesmaids adequately inferior. Comtesa Berzam stood nearby with her "medicine to calm her heart," and Marziah's Aunt Norris tried to cry but was really feeling too victorious at having manufactured such an advantageous attachment on behalf of her niece that tears just would not have been believable. Yes, marriage was a maneuvering business.

Chapter 19

For Femili, it soon became a daily exercise to find a way to avoid Hin'Rik Crawly. In order to accomplish this, she basically had to hide from everyone as he was always at Mansfield Park lately. She couldn't get away from him. And every day it was the same thing. The smiles, the compliments, the requests that she take him seriously. It was getting beyond annoying. There was absolutely nothing he could do that would change her opinion of him in her mind. Or so she thought.

After a few weeks of blunt, straightforward entreaties from Hin'Rik, he tried something different. Something that Femili would have never predicted.

The sound of her TelEx almost went unnoticed as she was not used to hearing it. There was no one besides Edwin who would contact her using the device and since he lived in the same house, he had no need to use it. But on this day, she received a TelEx from her beloved brother.

"My dear sister, I hope you are doing as well as I am right now."[describe how he looks] "You will never believe where I am." Wynn held the TelEx so that Femili could see a field with exercise equipment. She hadn't the faintest idea where he could be until she saw someone in uniform. The army! "That's right, I am on Engor. I have been accepted to the Engorian Army! I was scouted right from Minnith by a Senator Crawly."

Femili's smile faded. Senator Crawly? There was no way this was a coincidence.

"I am eternally grateful to the senator. He has set my military career on a trajectory that would have been unattainable on my own for at least another ten years. He told me to tell you something."

Here it comes, Femili thought.

"If you see his son, Hin'Rik, be sure to relay my

thanks and undying gratitude. Please Femili, show him any manner of kindness that you are able. He has really done our family a great service. My wages from the army will be able to ensure that our family never goes hungry again."

Femili didn't realize she was crying until she looked down and saw her dressing gown was wet with tears. On the one hand, she was so happy for Wynn and for her family. But on the other, she feared what Hin'Rik expected from her for his kindness. She wiped her tears away. It didn't matter. This was truly monumental aid to her family. She would be sure to thank him adequately and appropriately.

Just as she resolved in her heart to only see the purity in this gesture, she heard a knock on her door.

It was Hin'Rik.

"You are crying," he said with concern. "Why are you crying? What happened?"

She shook her head then wrapped her arms around him. "Thank you, Mr. Crawly."

"I take it you got a TelEx from your brother Wynn."

She nodded into his chest. "You have no idea what you have done for my family. I don't know how to thank you." She regretted those words as soon as they left her mouth. She had an idea of what he would request for a thank you. Now if he demanded she accept the mutual flirtation would she be able to reject him? Would she be obligated to accept him? Fortunately, that was not what he asked.

"If you want to thank me," he said, "do not ever call me Mr. Crawly again."

"What?" she asked, pulling away.

He pulled her close to him again and said, "Call me Hin'Rik."

"Okay."

"Seriously. I just want to hear my name in your sweet voice." He held her at arm's length and stared into her eyes. "Call me, Hin'Rik," he whispered.

"Thank you, Hin'Rik."

He smiled and said, "That is enough," before walking away.

***

Strategically, it was a waste, Hin'Rik thought to himself as he went down the stairs of Mansfield Park.

It had taken so much work and pleading and negotiating with his father in order for him to make the move to accept a half human into the Engorian army with the galaxy's most elite soldiers. After all that work, Hin'Rik traded it in merely for Femili to call him by his first name.

Why did he do that? It was so unlike him. But after a week of her avoiding him as if he had some sort of communicable disease, he really needed to hear her voice. And to hear her voice say his name was like fuel for his soul. He felt he could live another day.

Chapter 20

"Where are we headed?" Thom asked once they were aboard the guster.

Jason rolled his eyes. "Did you not check the itinerary?"

"If I did, would I be asking?"

"He doesn't need to," Mac said, coming to his defense. "He just needs to show up and punch things. That's what he's good at."

So she was coming to his defense, but she was also saying that he was only good at punching things. What did this mean? Was it good or bad? He honestly didn't know.

Jason sighed. "We're going to Tentor. There is

supposed to be a shipment of human girls leaving the planet headed for Revua tonight."

"We hope to intercept it before it takes off." Mac turned around and looked at Thom. "Then you can do what you do best."

Thom smiled. It felt like a compliment. She had complimented him. It meant she liked him. It had to. *Okay, Thom. Time to make a move*, he said to himself.

"Two minutes to landing," Jason said.

"I like you," Thom blurted.

"Sorry buddy. I just want to be friends."

"I think he was talking to me," Mac said.

"Well, he didn't specify. How am I supposed to know?"

"It's about time you told me how you feel, Thom," Mac said as she ignored her brother. "You've been following me around the galaxy for three years. I was beginning to think I was invisible to you."

"Can you guys please continue this later?" Jason said. "We are about to land and I need you focused. We each have a job here."

Jason started landing procedures as Mac took off her seat belt and stood up.

"What are you doing? We haven't landed," Jason said.

Mac stood in front of Thom's seat where he was apparently frozen with a mix of emotions. Poor AiJalonians really had no idea how to deal with their feelings. Mac leaned over and kissed Thom full on the lips. The guster lurched as Jason touched down, causing her to fall into Thom's lap. Mac smiled, then kissed him again. "It's about time you said so," she said again before standing and heading for the exit hatch.

"What a woman," was all Thom could say.

"Gross," was all Jason could say.

It was a standard mission based on intelligence that Mac had acquired from one of the parties she frequented. When she dressed up, Mac looked like the typical, shallow, and materialistic Lumercan elite. As such, people tended to have a very loose tongue with her once they had three or four drinks. She was able to find out any matter of information just by smiling at the right person. Everyone opened up to her. Maybe that was a blessing and a curse in Thom's eyes. It made him want to open up to her and tell her how he really felt, but it also made him doubt Mac's sincerity.

Was she really interested in him or was she just really good at her job of gathering intel? That explained why it literally took him three years to tell her. Now that he had though, he was immensely happy.

Gathering intel wasn't Mac Clintok's only job. She was also rather skilled with an equalizer. She could easily and accurately hit a target from up to fifty yards away. When the three of them worked together, Jason flew the spacecraft and took care of any medical emergencies. Thom handled the close contact hand-to-hand fighting as he led the girls to safety while Mac provided cover and offered backup if needed.

Today's mission flowed as planned. Mac actually felt it would go more smoothly than usual since she was now in a relationship with Thom. She felt she would be more observant and protect him even more than usual. But her feelings for him must have momentarily blinded her. She didn't see the danger that threatened him. And by the time she realized it, she was afraid it might have been too late.

Thom made quick work of the crew of the transport vessel that had the four young human girls slated for slavery. Seeing him effortlessly fight off three Harvothites made her heart swell.

Damn he was sexy. She only needed to fire off a couple of shots for his assistance. It was when he was on his way out of the vessel with the four girls in tow that she made her mistake.

Their three-person crew had begun to make a name for themselves throughout the galaxy. Because they were practically famous, many of the slave transport vessels sent additional reinforcements. That turned out to be the case today.

There were two reinforcement vessels, which meant nine additional men sent to protect this human cargo. And they were all armed. These girls must have been headed for very important clients. Normally, this wouldn't have been too much of a setback. Thom could handle nine men at once at least for a little while. And with Mac as a sniper, he should have been fine. But no one had prepared for their advanced technology.

Mac started emptying rounds of her equalizer into the cargo bay to protect her Thom. But it was almost as if she couldn't shoot fast enough. They had some sort of device that rendered her equalizer ineffective.

"Jason, get out here!" Her brother was a horrible shot so he wouldn't be able to help on that front. But maybe he would be able to change the settings on her equalizer to make them more effective. "Something's wrong," she said, handing him one of her equalizers while still shooting another.

"I'm on it," he said, getting to work on the settings. "They are using some sort of dampener I'm not familiar with. I can't fix it."

"Oh no," she said once she recognized the kaselray held by one of the armed men. It was similar to a nomaray that sent a pulse that knocked out power and living beings. The kaselray, however, only focused on living beings by temporarily paralyzing their central nervous system. It was especially effective on AiJalonians who tended to have more metal in their bloodstream than other species. "Thom, run!" she yelled, but it was too late. There was nowhere for him to go.

Mac couldn't wait for Jason to finish reprogramming her equalizer. She had to get to Thom before he was rendered immobile and at the mercy of these Harvothite henchmen. Mac grabbed a pipe from the floor and took out two of the men in a matter of seconds.

But it wasn't enough.

They launched the device, bringing Thom to his knees. And though he must have been in excruciating pain, he was cogniszant enough to recognize a whole in the fuel take about 10 feet away from him. A whole undoubtedly caused by one of her bullets. Thom managed to push the girls back into the vessel before the explosion that rendered everything silent. Mac felt her heart clench in her chest as she realized there was no way he could have survived.

Chapter 21

The Tentor police agency was notoriously slow an ineffective. Under normal circumstances Thom, Mac, and Jason would have stayed on the planet to insure that each of the girls safely returned to their home planet. There was no time for that in this instance. The girls were safe. But Thom was barely clinging on to life. The explosion had left his body burned and mangled. They had to get him advanced medical care immediately. The kind of care they could only find on Lumerca.

"Can you save him?" Mac asked her brother. "You have to save him. Please, Jason."

"Quiet. Let me work," he said. "Can you fly this thing

back to Oroton 4? I need my lab. There's so much ... "
Jason's voice caught in his throat as he realized the enormity
of the task in front of him. He had already inserted the blood
replicator to increase Thom's blood volume, but it would
have no effect if he didn't quickly stop the bleeding from his
friend's severed limbs. But once that was done, he needed to
check the internal damage. There was no telling how many
organs he would have to grow in his lab to replace the
damaged ones in Thom's body.

Mac sat in the pilot seat and fumbled with the controls
as she tried to mentally recall what Jason had done thousands
of times. She should have paid more attention.

"How is he?" Mac asked when she finally was able to
figure out the flight initiation sequence.

"He's fine." It was a lie. It was a complete lie. Jason
was just glad he didn't have any AiJalonian blood in him. It
would have been extremely inconvenient to not have the
ability to lie in this moment. He needed his sister calm so
that they could make it back to Oroton 4 in time.

Once they were in the air and the coordinates plugged
in, Mac left the pilot's seat and went to assist her brother.
"What can I do? What do you want me to do?"

Jason wanted her to just go back to the cockpit, but
the truth was he really did need her.

"Open my mobile med bay, take a sample of his blood, put it in the vial and then load it. Type in the following organs and limbs we need grown."

Mac obeyed. "How long will it take to get everything you need to save him?"

Jason made sure the life support system was fully engaged before answering. "If I pull some strings and call in some favors maybe we can find some black-market organs, but the limbs have to be grown to be completely compatible. We're looking at two weeks, ten days at the earliest."

"Can he live that long? What about my organs? Can you use mine?"

"Don't be ridiculous, Mac. You're human and Lumercan. They'll never match. Get on the holophone and make some calls for me. I need to open him up." Jason started slicing open Thom's chest.

"I'm going to puke!"

"Don't you dare!" Jason turned and slapped his sister in the face. "Get yourself together. I need you. He needs you."

She nodded furiously. "Okay. Okay. You're right." She sat down on the floor and set about making calls. "And just so you know. That is the first and last time you will ever slap me without repercussions," she said.

"Noted."

Jason made the tough decision to go back to Oroton 4 instead of Lumerca proper. It would have been easier to get the organs he needed on Lumerca, but his lab and equipment were on the Lumercan moon. Besides he could send Mac to Lumerca to get what he needed. It would be a good distraction for her so she wouldn't be in the way, crying her eyes out. He had never seen his sister cry so much in their entire lives. It was only the years of training he had received in the medical academy that helped him keep it together and work on saving his friend. If he had focused on the fact that it was actually Thom nearly dead on the table, his best friend and the man his sister loved, he would have completely lost it.

What kind of poetic injustice was it that as soon as they had finally made progress on their relationship this tragedy struck? It wasn't fair.

He and Mac had suffered enough in their lives. At least one of them deserved a chance at happiness. There was not a chance in hell he would let Thom Berzam die.

"How's your ankle?" Jason asked when Mac entered his lab. She had just returned from her third trip to Lumerca to purchase supplies.

"It's fine," she said, making her way right back to Thom's bedside.

"Do you need me to take a look at it?"

"I already set the bone myself. And I'm pretty well hopped up on painkillers right now so, like I said, I'm fine." She sat down next to the pressurized tube that encapsulated her Thom and was breathing for him, longing to be able to hold his hand in hers. But he didn't even have one at the moment. The next time she could hold his hand she promised she'd never let it go. "If you ask me about my ankle one more time or send me on another worthless trip to Lumerca to get me out of your hair, I swear to Gaion I will kick you in the nuts until they are lodged in your throat."

"You don't even believe in Gaion," was Jason's response to her empty threat. He knew she didn't mean it. At this point, he was the last person she would harm as he was the only one who could save Thom.

"If he lives, I'll start," she said.

Chapter 22

Twenty-three days. It had been twenty-three days since Hin'Rik had confessed his feelings for her. Femili thought by now he'd be tired of this game, but he wasn't. He had even gone so far as to involve her brother. And while she did appreciate his help in getting Wynn into the army, that act had not moved her heart toward him. She just could not accept him.

Instead of tiring of his pursuit, he seemed to be even more driven to succeed. Every rejection from Femili just made him work harder to gain her approval. It had long past annoyance from Femili's point of view and was now entering into complete misery.

Every day after finishing her household chores, she

retreated to her room which turned out to be the only safe space away from Hin'Rik Crawly.

Normally, it was Edwin who comforted her when she needed it. And she needed it now as Hin'Rik was completely stressing her out. But Edwin declined to be by her side and she knew why. She knew very well why they needed to stay away from each other. Thus, she hadn't even seen him in days as he had locked himself in his quarters to study for his entrance exam into the Orthodox Miniran Order.

When she returned to her room on the afternoon of the twenty-fourth day of Hin'Rik Crawly's occupation of Mansfield Park, a call from her uncle was waiting for her.

"So is it all settled then?" his hologram asked her.

"Is what all settled?" she asked.

"You and Mr. Crawly. He called me today and formally asked for your hand. I have to tell you I quite admire him. Even with your humanity, he still put in the effort to make a formal request for you. What a gentleman."

Femili was silent as Comte Berzam rambled on about all of Hin'Rik's fine qualities.

"Well?" he asked when Femili didn't respond. "Is it all settled? The flirtation that is. From how Hin'Rik speaks about you, I am not surprised that it was a short flirtation. I think we can schedule a wedding for next Amaven. I know

Hin'Rik is rather eager."

"I'm sure he is," Femili said to herself.

"What was that? Speak clearly, child."

She sighed. "Yes, it is quite settled."

"Oh, good."

"I will never accept Hin'Rik Crawly. I never even agreed to a mutual flirtation."

After noticing the fierce look in her uncle's eyes, Femili was very happy that her uncle was in hologram form and not there in the flesh. She did a few mental calculations in her mind to make sure that being smacked by a hologram was still scientifically impossible.

"What do you mean?" he asked incredulously.

She said it again in Ancient Ai.

"Are you mocking me and the AiJalonian culture?"

"Absolutely not, sir."

Comte Berzam took a breath and tried to remain calm. "Maybe you are unclear on what a mutual flirtation is. You did grow up on Minnith. I can assure you it is completely innocent and proper."

"I know what it is, uncle."

"Well, maybe it is too innocent and proper for you since you are a human. But once you get married you can carry out your human fleshly cravings all you want."

"That is not the issue."

"Well, what is the issue?"

"I don't like him. Nay, I despise him."

Seething with anger, Comte Berzam took several deep breaths. "And this is how you repay me for the years of benevolence I have shown you?"

"If I had known that I would have to repay your kindness by marrying a man that truly disgusts me, I never would have agreed to live at Mansfield Park." Femili instantly regretted speaking to her uncle in this manner. He really had shown her an undeserved kindness by letting her live there for the past three years. But the daily stress of having to avoid Hin'Rik Crawly had finely worn her patience away. She couldn't take it anymore.

"If this is the way you feel, I think you may need a reminder of the poverty from which I saved you. You are to return to Minnith immediately."

"Gladly."

"And don't think of returning until you are ready to accept Hin'Rik Crawly as your mate."

"In that case, I suppose this is goodbye forever, uncle."

Chapter 23

Yes, Minnith was a poor planet of priests and Femili's family was probably one of the poorest, but after a week at home, she still didn't regret her decision. She could finally breathe, free from the outright stalking of Hin'Rik Crawly. Unfortunately, that freedom did not last long.

"Femmy, you have a visitor," her mother called exactly eight days after her return.

"A visitor?" she looked a question at her sister.

Suiana shrugged.

"He must be from AiJalon. He's in a very expensive tobulon."

"Maybe it's Edwin?" Suiana asked

At the mere thought that her Edwin could have traveled the galaxy just to visit her, Femili threw on her frock and nearly fell as she stepped over siblings to enter the main room. But it wasn't Edwin who awaited her. Disappointment settled in her stomach like an indigestible stone as she stared into the face of Hin'Rik Crawly.

"What are you doing here?" Her voice was filled with defeat as if she had just lost a battle.

"Femili, don't be so rude," her mother said. "He is our guest."

"It's quite all right, ma'am," Hin'Rik said with his dashing grin. "Even her rudeness is adorable. I have missed it desperately."

Femili rolled her eyes and sighed.

After much cajoling from her mother, Femili finally relented and agreed to go on a walk with Hin'Rik.

"Seriously, why are you here?" Femili asked again once they were alone. "No lies. No excuses. Just the truth."

Hin'Rik stopped walking. Turning toward her, he said, "I need you to listen to me very carefully."

"Okay," she said with an exasperated sigh.

"No. I hear it in your voice. You are not listening to

me. I need you to take my words deep inside you. I don't need you to answer or just tell me what I want to hear. But I do need you to take my words in with half as much care as I am giving them to you."

Femili nodded, slightly taken aback by the sincerity of his voice.

"I am a bad person," he began. Femili forced herself to not nod in furious agreement. "I drink too much. I lie. I cheat. I have had many women. And I have never regretted any of it. Not until I met you." He grabbed her hand and brought it to his chest. "You have touched me in a way that no other woman ever has. You are engraved on my heart, my mind, and my soul. I no longer only think about myself because all there is, is you. I love you, Femili Primme. I love you more than I have loved anyone or anything in my life. If you say you'll love me back ... No. Just say you'll *try* to love me back. That's all I need. Just try to love me as much as I love you and I promise to make you the happiest woman in the galaxy."

"I ... I ... " She wasn't sure how to respond. She knew she didn't love him. She wasn't sure if she ever could love him. But she couldn't help but be moved by his confession. Any feeling person would be.

"Does not your religion teach about redemption? Can't anyone be forgiven for past acts through your savior? Why should I be treated any differently? Why can you not try to see past what I was and see what I am trying to be?"

Femili still couldn't respond for several moments. She felt the beating of his heart under her palm and was momentarily hypnotized. That was the only explanation for what she said next. "I'll try."

Hin'Rik's eyes expanded as he gripped her hand even tighter. "You didn't say no." His voice was almost a whisper as if he was shocked by the words coming out of his own mouth. "This is the first time you haven't rejected me outright."

Femili nodded. "I am not rejecting you outright. But I am also not accepting you," she said.

Hin'Rik pulled her close to him and hugged her. "That's all I ask. Just give me a chance to move your heart toward me. You won't regret it."

***

Much to Femili's surprise, Hin'Rik stayed on Minnith. She could not imagine that he was even remotely comfortable with the accommodations offered. For even the most expensive room on Minnith was probably equivalent to a shack on his home planet of Engor.

But he stayed and never complained or seemed the slightest bit unhappy. Quite to the contrary, each day he seemed to glow with delight in the presence of Femili as he helped her with housework, or gardening, or shopping, or any of the enormity of duties she was tasked with while at home.

Every day in the early afternoon, the sky above the Eastern hemisphere of Minnith glowed in hues of orange and pink due to the gases in their atmosphere and the planet's rotation around a Lumercan sun.

The Bongwhan religion on the planet named this part of the day "The Hour of Transcendence." They taught that during this hour the gods of love and war called a truce and allowed a peace to blossom between former enemies. It was thought of as the best time to apologize, to settle arguments, or ask for a favor. The mythology behind this time of day was no doubt the reason Femili's parents would give her a respite from her duties and virtually kick her out the house to a waiting Hin'Rik. After several days of this routine, Hin'Rik and Femili naturally started walking side-by-side without even exchanging words of introduction.

"I'm sorry I was late," Hin'Rik said on one such walk.

Femili looked at the sky to estimate the time. "No, you are exactly on time."

"No, I don't mean today. I mean late to this planet. I missed the third of the month."

"Oh," she said thinking back to over a month ago when they had met at the lake. He remembered her night terrors.

"I tried to get here precisely on that day, but as it turns out, I had a rather difficult time convincing my father to let me leave AiJalon."

"Why will he not let you leave a planet that is not even your own?"

Hin'Rik stopped walking and looked at the sky for a moment, seeming to gather his thoughts. "I was exiled to AiJalon after committing some nefarious deeds on Engor. I would rather not get into the details, but if you ask, I will answer. I cannot deny any request from you, small or large."

"I see." Femili saw the pain in his eyes and he suddenly wasn't as disgusting to her as he was before. What was happening to her? Damn hour of transcendence! "I ... I don't really need to know any details."

"Thank you." He started walking again. "So were you all right that evening?" he asked, quickly changing the subject.

Femili thought for a moment. The third of the month came and went without incident. She hadn't even thought about it until Hin'Rik brought it up. She explained this to Hin'Rik.

"That is odd," he said. "Does it have something to do with AiJalon itself? It must."

Femili nodded silently.

"In any case," Hin'Rik continued, "I am glad you are well." He reached for her hand and she actually considered taking it. No, no, she thought to herself. *This man is a sex-crazed scoundrel who is putting on a false face with me.* She would not fall for his charms. But then again, he had been tirelessly consistent. Maybe, just maybe ... No. She shook off the thought, resisted the urge to take his hand, and continued walking.

"Has your heart moved even a little?" he asked her once they reached the end of the path they were currently on.

"I am not sure."

"I think it has," he said, taking a step closer to her. "If it hadn't, you would not let me stand this close to you. You are too pure. I am almost afraid that my sins will somehow rub off on you."

Hin'Rik brought his hand to her face and caressed her cheek. She didn't swat it away. Taking the lack of resistance as encouragement, he slowly traced the lines of her lips with his thumb. "In truth, one kiss from you could almost definitely cleanse all my sins like holy water from an angel of Gaion."

Femili felt her breath catch in her chest. Hin'Rik Crawly always claimed that she had a way with words, but he was definitely an expert in his own right. Was that because he had practiced such sweet words on multiple women before? She knew she was just next in his line of conquests. Or did she? Was it possible that he did truly love her and was his love slowly opening her heart up to him?

"May I kiss you, Femili Primme?"

"Yes." She didn't remember saying the word but she definitely heard the word and in her own voice.

It wasn't his first kiss, but it might as well have been. He felt sensations in his body that he had never felt before. Her lips entranced him and enflamed every fiber of his being. How did she have so much power over him? In his mind, every other kiss would forever be in two categories. Before Femili and after Femili.

After the kiss, he was forced to stare at her for a moment to make sure she was an actual physical being and not a mystical creature sent from above to control him. He caressed the side of her face and touched her lips again with his thumb, aching for the moment their lips would touch again. "Femili," he said.

"Yes?"

"You may not know it yet, but you are growing to love me. I felt it. I felt your body respond to me."

Femili averted her eyes as if she wanted to hide the truth.

"I have to go," she said awkwardly wiggling out of his embrace and nearly running away. He let her go. His point had been made. She would be completely his soon.

Was he sincere in his feelings toward Femili Primme? She was a poor half-breed with no social standing or connection. She would not be able to advance his career or add to his finances. But for the first time in his life, he didn't care. That was sincerity, wasn't it? He honestly didn't know. It was a word, an emotion that he not only had never felt before but had honestly never even thought of before. What he did know was that he had to have her. He had to make her his any way he could.

Chapter 24

The kiss had taken their relationship to another level. Hin'Rik knew that if he had just a few more days alone with her on Minnith, she would be completely his. Even the evening after the kiss, he caught her staring at him in a way that she had never done before. And before he retired to his lodging for the night, she let him hug her. Femili was starting to see him in a new light. He truly felt the gods of Minnith were helping him.

The next day he had planned to make it his mission to hold her hand as they walked and to, of course, kiss her again. But his plans were thwarted.

"I have to go back to Mansfield Park," she said.

"Why?" he asked.

"I just heard from my Aunt Berzam. Thom is severely injured and she needs me."

Hin'Rik took her hand. "She absolutely does not need you. Mansfield Park has medical droids. Your aunt has Ju'Lya, Marziah and her husband, and your Aunt Norris. What could she possibly need you for?"

"I happen to be a calming presence on Mansfield Park."

He pulled her into an embrace. "You are a calming presence on me," he said after kissing her cheek.

She pushed him away slightly. "I should go."

"Why? Aren't we happy here? And you still have not given me an answer. Can I have your heart?"

Femili couldn't answer that question. It was impossible. She felt her heart belonged to someone else. She couldn't give it away if she tried. But how was she supposed to explain that to Hin'Rik?

"I feel like I am in a dreamworld with you here, Femili. Going back to AiJalon ... I don't know ... I just think it would feel like waking up. I don't want to wake up. Not yet."

"Why not? Do you not trust yourself?"

Honestly, he did not. Here on Minnith there was

nothing to distract his gaze from his Femili. Literally nothing. It was hands down the most boring planet in the galaxy, worse than AiJalon. He tried to have confidence in the love he felt for her, but he couldn't be sure of himself.

Femili shook her head. "What am I even doing with you? I can't trust you. I cannot do this anymore."

"After all this time, you still don't trust me?" It was a ridiculous question. She had every reason not to trust him, especially since he didn't even trust himself. He took a deep, calming breath. "Don't answer that, Femili. I know you too well. I can see it in your eyes. But I will not give up. We can continue this courtship on AiJalon."

"This isn't a courtship, Hin'Rik. I don't know what it is, but ... I'm sorry. I just can't. Every time I look at you, I just see Marziah and Ju'Lya. How are we supposed to start a relationship like this?"

"So that is what your resistance is about? You are jealous of the attention that I showed them. Well, when we get back to AiJalon, I will correct that. I will make it clear that you are the only one for me. It was a mistake to fool with their emotions. I never felt for them what I feel for you."

Hin'Rik deeply regretted ever being involved with that ridiculous game with his sister. But that was in the past. He was confident that he would be able to show his Femili that he was a changed man. And that she was the one that had changed him.

Thom's condition was worse than she could have ever imagined. He was basically an unconscious torso and head. And though the human doctor that never left his side seemed optimistic, Femili was unsure. She had never seen anyone recover from injuries so severe. But then again, she had lived on Minnith her entire life. She was not used to the advanced medical techniques that were available on Lumerca. The human doctor and the Lumercan woman with him had spared no expense in his recovery. From what Femili had overheard, Thom's spleen, pancreas, liver, and left lung had all been replaced. Also, his right foot, left leg below the knee, left arm below the elbow, and right hand were currently being grown on Lumerca. Femili knew it was possible to do such things, but she had never met anyone who actually had a lab-grown appendage. Soon her cousin would have four.

Back in Mansfield Park, her main duty wasn't actually helping to take care of her cousin. The human doctor, Jason, and his Lumercan assistant Mac were on hand to do that. No, Femili was actually there to take care of Comtesa Berzam. Her nerves were so shot at seeing the state of her son that she had been continuously drinking tonics and taking tranquilizers. The family was so afraid that she might end up in a state of unconsciousness that Femili was there to monitor her intake of medication and make sure she didn't overdose.

During her stay on Minnith, Edwin and Meril had apparently gotten much closer. They were practically inseparable, always speaking quietly to one another. Was this part of the Crawly plan? Had Hin'Rik and Meril intentionally sought out to disrupt the attachment between her and Edwin? Maybe that was the real reason Hin'Rik had come to Minnith. Femili shook off the thought. There was no way Hin'Rik and Meril even knew about the love she felt for Edwin and he for her.

Hin'Rik returned to AiJalon with Meril and stayed around Mansfield Park most days. Or maybe he didn't. Honestly, Femili was too busy to inquire about his whereabouts most of the time. Every once in a while, she got a glimpse of him looking sullen and lonely. Probably because he felt he wasn't getting sufficient attention. But she already had a patient in her Aunt Berzam. She didn't have time to also nurse Hin'Rik's bruised ego.

Three days after Thom, and subsequently Femili,

returned to Mansfield Park, Marziah also returned with her new husband, Mr. Rushworth. She really wasn't needed, but Femili got the feeling that Marziah was trying to escape newlywed time with her husband. And for some reason, it seemed like Marziah was more interested in Hin'Rik than her own brother.

Femili made it a habit to visit her aunt's quarters around three o'clock in the morning just to check on her. It was usually around this time of the early morning that her medication from the previous night wore off and she was looking for more. Femili would try to give her some less-addictive medicinal herbs from Minnith instead of more drugs. Most nights it worked, but others she was not so fortunate.

On one particular night a week after her return to Mansfield Park, Femili was making her way back to her room after visiting her aunt when she heard moaning coming from the parlor. Common sense should have told her not to investigate, but curiosity was a powerful motivator. Truth be told, she half expected to see Edwin and Meril in some sort of compromising position. Maybe if she saw that, it would help put an end to the lingering feelings she had for him. It was worth a try. Unfortunately, she did not catch Edwin and

Meril in a lover's embrace. Instead, it was Hin'Rik and Marziah.

Hin'Rik's chest was bare and not even covered by a bodysuit. Marziah was in an even further state of undress. It was pure skin to skin contact. If she had been caught like this by her husband, he would be granted an immediate divorce with full propriety.

"What is this?" All eyes turned to a surprised Mr. Rushworth exiting the dining room with a slice of bread in his hands. "Wife?" he asked, looking back and forth between Marziah and Hin'Rik. Marziah quickly pulled her dress up to cover herself as her husband turned and started up the stairs while asking himself if he was dreaming. "I don't think I'm dreaming. I can taste this bread and it is very flavorful. Why would I be dreaming about this?"

From across the room, Femili locked eyes with Hin'Rik. They stared at each other in silence. Femili refused to be the first one to look away. She had done nothing to be ashamed of.

"Femili, what are you doing here at this time of night?" he asked.

"First of all, it is morning, not night. Second of all, I live here. And third and perhaps the more relevant question is what are *you* doing here at this hour, *Mrs*. Rushworth?"

"That is none of your concern!" Clutching her dress to her chest, Marziah ran past Femili, presumably in pursuit of her husband.

"Femili, listen to me," Hin'Rik said once Marziah had left the room.

"Why should I listen to anything you have to say?"

"This was all Marziah. She planned this. She must have known you would be up at this hour."

"So either you are dumb enough to fall for a plot from Marziah or you don't care for me enough to control your fleshly desires?"

"Please don't say that. Please don't doubt that I love you."

"Then, what is it?"

"I don't know. I'm Engorian. I have needs. Needs that you haven't—"

"We're done here," Femili said, interrupting him. She left the parlor and walked towards Comtesa Berzam's quarters.

Hin'Rik caught up with her before she entered the room. "I'm sorry, okay. I'm sorry," he said. "Do you hear me, Femili? I have never apologized to anyone in my life. But I am apologizing to you. I am sorry that I was too weak to thwart her advances. I am sorry that I am such a lowlife. I am sorry that I am not perfect like you." He grabbed her arm and pulled her to him.

"Let me go, Hin'Rik."

"No. I can't. Please let me try again," he begged.

"Let me go!"

"The lady wants you to let her go," Edwin said as he exited his mother's room.

"This doesn't concern you, Edwin. We're just having a lover's quarrel."

"Everything dealing with Femili concerns me," he said. Femili felt her heart swell. "You don't live here. I suggest you leave." Edwin, by nature, did not have a very intimidating stature, but in that moment, even Femili was a little intimidated by the ferocity in his voice. Hin'Rik apparently felt he shouldn't take up this fight at the moment. He relinquished Femili's arm and retreated. "Femmy," Edwin said, turning his attention to his cousin.

Femili hadn't realized the emotional toll this entire encounter had had on her until Hin'Rik was finally gone. She collapsed into Edwin's chest. Slowly, he wrapped his arms around her. She felt at home and at peace. The mere seconds she spent in his embrace were the happiest she'd felt the entire past month.

"Edwin," she said as tears began to escape her eyes.

"Shh. It's okay. He's gone. He's not going to hurt you."

Femili shook her head. "No, that's not it. That is not why I am crying." She looked up at him. "I can't believe how much I missed you."

"Oh, Femmy." He wiped her tears away with his thumbs as he cradled her head in his hands. One kiss wouldn't hurt anyone, he told himself. Just one.

But one kiss led to another and then another. Then suddenly, they were at the door to Edwin's room.

"Femmy, if you come into my room, I think we both know what will happen."

Femili rested her head on his just and listened to his accelerated heart rate and heavy breathing for a moment. She closed her eyes and imagined what the rest of the day would look like if she gave in to her sinful, fleshly desires in this moment. She couldn't do it. And she hated herself for it. She pushed him away and retreated to her room.

Chapter 25

"Where is my son?" Comte Berzam said as he burst through the doors of Mansfield Park. He followed a medical droid to the makeshift hospital room that Mac and Jason had created. Between Jason's medical expertise and Mac's obvious money and connections, the most state-of-the-art medical facility on the planet of AiJalon was currently in Mansfield Park. "What happened to him?" he asked once he was next to Thom. He had to swallow back the bile that had entered into his mouth upon seeing his son in such a state.

"I know he looks bad, Comte Berzam," Jason began, "but, internally, he is stable and almost as good as new. Externally, he will be back to normal sooner than you can imagine."

"His missing body parts are almost done," Mac said. "I will pick them up from Lumerca in two days."

"What happened to him?" Comte Berzam repeated.

Tears welled in Mac's eyes once again. Jason was surprised she had any more tears left. He knew she would hardly be able to talk about what happened without breaking down so he decided to answer the question. "We ran into some difficulty on Tentor."

"Tentor? What was he doing on Tentor?" Comte Berzam asked. "He told me he was going to Lumerca. And who are you people? Why is he cavorting with a human on a human planet?"

Tentor wasn't a completely human planet. Yes, it did have the highest human population of any of the other planets in the galaxy, but they still weren't the majority species. Strictly speaking, the only human planet was Earth and that had been abandoned centuries ago. Jason, however, did not feel it was time to correct Comte Berzam on his galactic anthropology. Instead, he had to figure out a way to answer him in a satisfactory manner. Did he reveal what Thom did in his spare time? Is that what he would have wanted? Or did he lie to his friend's father, something that he was perfectly equipped to do as a human?

"He was there because of me," Mac volunteered, fighting back her tears.

"And who are you?"

"Mac Clintok of the Tabor clan of Lumerca."

Comte Berzam paused for a moment as his mind mentally reviewed the Lumercan clans. Tabor was rather high. The woman before him, despite her meager appearance, was filthy rich. She could literally buy and sell Mansfield Park several times over. That answer was enough to quench his curiosity for the time being. He still didn't know why his son was on Tentor getting blown up, but knowing he was with a Tabor clan member had to mean there was at least a good reason. Perhaps Thom was looking to forge a business connection with them. In any case, Comte Berzam didn't ask any further questions about the why and instead focused on what needed to be done to restore his son to perfect health.

Mac's social status once again saved the day. Between Thom's natural instincts and Mac's connections and finances, they made such a great team. Jason just hoped they would be able to continue working together. First, Thom had to survive.

After having his medical questions answered by Jason

and learning about Thom's way to recovery, Comte Berzam retreated to the parlor where he had Femili bring him a glass of Gadolan rum.

"I'll have one too, Femili," Comtesa Berzam said.

"Are you sure that will not have a negative reaction with your medication?" Aunt Norris asked.

"My son is on death's door. I need something to steady my nerves."

Femili obeyed but made sure to give Comtesa Berzam a mere half a glass. She too was worried about the effects of her aunt's medication.

Moments later, Edwin entered with Meril on his arm. *Were they official?* Femili asked to herself. Had they entered into a mutual flirtation? How could he do that after they had just kissed? Again. Or maybe it was *because* they had just kissed. He was running away from his feelings. He was running away from Femili right into the arms of Meril. Femili took a deep breath and tried not to focus on what could never be. Maybe Meril and Edwin would be good together.

"Where are Marziah and Rushworth?" Comte Berzam asked once he had finished his glass. "Shouldn't they be here while Thom is in this state?"

A heavy silence fell over the room as everyone desperately tried to avoid Comte Berzam's eyes. "What? What is it?" he asked.

No one answered. "Femili, speak. What has happened?"

"I don't think I am the best to—"

"There was an incident early this morning," Meril interrupted. Femili was quite thankful for the interruption as she didn't want to have to be the one to tell her uncle what his daughter had done.

Edwin continued, "Hin'Rik and Marziah were caught in a state of undress by Mr. Rushworth and Femili."

Comte Berzam flopped down into a seat as if he no longer had the energy to stand. "Femili, is this true?"

Femili nodded.

"Gaion, above! What curse has befallen Mansfield Park?"

"Does it really have to be a curse?" Meril began as everyone slowly turned their heads to her, wondering where she was going with this line of questioning. "I mean, they are both passionate people. They are actually quite well-suited for each other. Perhaps they will be happy together."

"Happy together?" Comte Berzam asked. "You mean it is decided? Rushworth will not take her back?"

"Well, after Femili rejected my brother once again, he and Marziah left together to head to Cosmo. My inclination is to believe that they plan on making a go of their relationship."

"After Femili rejected him?" Comte Berzam asked incredulously. "It seems as if Femili rightly rejected him. It seems as if she is the only one who accurately calculated his true character and judged him accordingly."

"Perhaps," Meril said as she stood and began to meander around the room, capturing the attention of everyone. "Femili, being as wise and good as she is, has always been an excellent judge of character I suspect. She certainly did have the proper assessment of my brother. But, on the other hand, though he is somewhat of a knave by AiJalonian standards, it is possible that the innocence and purity of one Femili Primme could have righted his wayward course. We may never know what kind of man he could have turned out to be if he had been paired with her as he so desperately wished."

"It is not Femili's obligation nor responsibility to cleanse the character of another—" Comte Berzam stated.

"But," Meril said, interrupting him, "that is neither here nor there. We will never know. We can only deal with the situation we have at hand. And what do we have? Hin'Rik and Marziah will be married, I am sure, as soon as her divorce is finalized. And we have an ill elder son in Thom. Should, Gaion forbid, Thom pass away, his fifty percent inheritance would then pass on to Edwin. Because of Marziah's less than appropriate second attachment, her inheritance will pass on to Edwin as well, giving him five sixths of the estate. With that sum of money, he has no need to go into the priesthood. He can marry well, establish himself in AiJalonian society and then welcome Hin'Rik and Marziah back with open arms. All will soon be forgotten."

"And who did you have in mind for this suitable marriage mate for myself?" Edwin asked, a hint of anger dangling from his words.

"Edwin?" Meril was surprised by his tone. She had no idea what in her words could have possibly offended him. She thought she had given a very reasonable and sensible plan. The prospective marriage mate for himself should have been obvious. Having a slight fortune in his possession was the only way someone with her Engorian stature could possibly marry him.

She was doing him a favor by even offering this possibility. Truth be told, she was delighted to do so. She could actually now picture herself being married to Edwin.

Thom and Marziah simultaneously relinquishing their fortunes to him was almost too perfect to be true.

"You have insulted me, my siblings and generally everyone in the Berzam family."

"How did ... I don't ... "

"Must my marriage to you be predicated upon the death of my brother and the impropriety of my sister? How could you possibly think I would delight in the union with someone who relishes such topics?"

"Oh, Edwin, I didn't mean it that way."

"Well, it sure sounded like it. And then on top of you virtually wishing death on my brother, you imbue bad intentions to myself. You suggest that I would give up the priesthood merely for money. Lady, you do not know me at all and I wish not to know you further. Please leave at once."

"Edwin, I ... " Meril looked around the room for possible reinforcements and met only blank or angry stares. "Femili, you must know this was not my sentiment," she pleaded with Femili.

"I cannot dare to venture a guess as to the motive of your words. Merely to think such a thing is a disgrace. To voice them ... " Femili shook her head. "I have to agree with Edwin. You need to leave. At once."

Chapter 26

Femili watched from a distance as Edwin stared silently at a Centauri Fichus in the conservatory. She didn't know what he was thinking, but she was sure that he wasn't in the best of moods after his falling out with Meril. She wanted to talk to him and comfort him, but she wasn't sure what to do or say.

"Are you just going to stare at me for the rest of the day?" he said suddenly.

She stepped out of the shadows and approached him. "I didn't know you knew I was here."

"I heard you enter twenty minutes ago." He continued to look at the plant and spoke without turning his head.

She didn't respond. She wasn't sure how to.

"I'm fine, by the way," he said. Femili knew he was lying even without noticing how he had involuntarily convulsed. He wasn't fine. He seemed like he was about to do something drastic. "I'm leaving for the monastery today."

And there it was. Something drastic.

"What?" Femili didn't know why she was so surprised. She knew this was what he had been preparing for. It was bound to happen one day. She just thought she would have a little more time with him.

"I can't stay here."

"If this is about Meril—"

"This is about you," he said, looking at her for the first time.

"Edwin, you—"

"We almost didn't stop ourselves last night."

Femili stared at the ground, guiltily recalling how one kiss had led to another and then another.

"I can't be near you anymore," he said, turning away.

Femili swallowed down a well of tears. "Edwin, now is not the time to leave your family. What about Thom? You can't do this to your parents."

"My parents are precisely why I must do this." He faced her again. "What happens if I get arrested for indecency while Thom is at death's door?" He took a step closer to her. "And don't make me think about what would happen to you. All because I can't control my urges. I wouldn't be able to live with the guilt."

Unable to speak for fear she would burst into tears, she just nodded while keeping her gaze on the ground. She understood what he was doing and why. And, honestly, she couldn't see a better option either.

"I leave in a few minutes," he said. "This is our goodbye."

***

Femili tried not to dwell on Edwin's abrupt departure. Instead, she focused on helping her aunt and even tried to assist the human doctor who had arrived with Thom.

"I'm not just any doctor. I'm Jason Barvery, youngest human graduate of the IMA," he was saying as they looked out on the lake together the next day. The doctor was taking a well needed break after over thirty straight hours next to Thom's side in the makeshift hospital they created in Mansfield Park.

He had probably been by his side even longer than that before they arrived at AiJalon. Femili was still unclear as to the what, when, and why of Thom's accident.

Femili looked at him strangely.

"The IMA is the Intergalactic Medical Academy," he added, thinking that was the reason for the strange look.

"Yes, I know what it is," Femili said, still confused as to why he felt the need to tell her this ... again. "I noticed you always specify *human* graduate. That must mean someone else has taken the overall youngest title."

His smile faded. "So, you are the half-human cousin from Minnith?" Jason asked, changing the subject. Truth be told, he wasn't quite over it and didn't want to dwell on that Revuan punk who stole his title.

Instead, he would focus on the mysterious Femili Primme who had captured Thom's attention. It was the first time since he had come to Mansfield Park that Jason had left Thom's side. Feeling that he was stable enough and wanting to give his sister some alone time with him, he decided to take a walk and had run into Femili at the lake.

She looked at him as if weighing his motives. "Yes," she said finally. "Why do you ask?"

Staring at her oddly he said, "Because once again I think Thom's instincts are correct." He turned and looked out over the lake. "I don't know how he did it. But he always made such astute evaluations in any situation. Once on Capernica, he was able to identify our target before he had even said a word. I really don't know how he missed the ambush on Tentor." If Jason was being honest with himself, he had a pretty good guess as to why. It was his sister, Mac. Thom was so distracted by his feelings for her that he was off his game. He couldn't sense the danger that he normally would have. Mac knew it was true as well, which was part of the reason she was so distraught. She felt Thom's condition was her fault. She would never forgive herself if he died. Jason was not going to let that happen.

"What exactly do you do with my cousin?"

Jason came to his senses. He had said too much. What was he thinking? He cleared his throat and said, "We are an intergalactic messenger service."

Femili was incredulous. "That was a terrible lie. Especially for a human."

"Yes, not my best," he said with a smile and a nod. "What gave it away?"

"Well, the delivery was adequate. But the content was ridiculous. Thom is AiJalonian nobility. Why would he ever find the need to deliver packages across the galaxy?"

"I usually tell that lie to people who do not know Thom."

"Well, then you may be safe as long as people do not recognize the Lumercan wealth rings on your friend Mac."

"You are extremely observant. Is that an AiJalonian trait or just something both you and Thom possess?"

Femili shrugged. "I am not sure. I have only lived on AiJalon for three years and in that time, I have not gotten to know many people outside of the Berzams and the ... Crawlys."

They both stopped talking for a moment and stared over the lake, each lost in their own thoughts.

"I can't quite put my finger on it, but you remind me of someone," Jason said finally. "I've been thinking it since the first time I saw you. You look like someone I've met before and now, talking to you, you seem even more familiar."

"I do have nine siblings. Have you ever been to Minnith? Maybe you've met one of them." Femili meant it as a joke, but Jason was not laughing.

"Do any of them look like you?"

Femili shook her head. "I take after my mother's AiJalonian side. My siblings look more human."

"Hmm," was all Jason said in response. "I am going to ask you something very personal. Please do not be offended."

"All right. I'll try."

"May I have your DNA?"

Femili was quite unsure of what Jason was doing or what he hoped to find with her DNA sample. She just sat back and watched as the medical droid did its analysis. Moments later, Jason read the results.

"He was right. Thom was right once again."

"Right about what?" Femili asked.

Jason turned to her and said, "You're not human. Not even a little bit."

She felt like the wind had been knocked out of her. Jason grabbed her arm and helped her to a seat in the guest bedroom that he had converted to a makeshift lab and medical facility.

"So, my father is not my father?"

Jason sighed. "I have an even bigger shock for you," he said.

Femili looked up at him with eyes filled with confusion and anticipation. What could be more of a shock than finding out she wasn't human after eighteen years and that the man who had loved and raised her for those eighteen years was not her father? What did this mean? Was her mother married before? Did she cheat on her father? What was happening?

"Are you ready?"

She nodded.

"Your mother is not your mother."

***

Normally, one would not be able to tell someone's parents through a quick medical droid test. They would usually need samples from the parents to compare with the child. But this situation was different. A quick glance at the results and even a first-year medical academy student could recognize the lack of human DNA. The structures were completely different. And because Jason had just spent the last two weeks knee-deep in Thom's DNA as he was trying to regrow so many organs and limbs, he could recognize the pattern and see that there was no overlap with Femili's DNA.

If Thom's aunt who happened to be his mother's twin sister was actually Femili's mother, there would have been an overlapping pattern. There was not. Just to be sure, while Femili was passed out from the shock, he ran a test of comparison between Femili and Thom. They were not related. Who exactly was this girl? Where did she come from? And who had decided to hide her identity for eighteen years? Given Jason's line of work in rescuing trafficked girls, he couldn't let this mystery slide.

"I just had the oddest dream," Femili said as she

awakened on Jason's table. "I dreamed my parents had been lying to me my entire life."

"It wasn't a dream," Jason said, staring at his TelEx. "You are not human in any way, shape or form and you are also not related to the Berzams."

Now that the initial shock had worn off, the realization of those words started to settle in. Yes, there would be a reckoning with her parents. They would have some explaining to do. But at this second, it wasn't what was important. She wasn't related to Edwin. That was the important part of this revelation. They could be together. "Edwin. I need to find Edwin." Femili stood up and headed for the door.

Jason grabbed her by the arm. "He left for Minnith already. He is headed for the monastery and will not be able to leave for three months. You know this."

"But maybe if I leave now and have a really fast guster … "

Jason shook his head. "There is no guster in existence that can travel that distance fast enough."

Femili started breathing heavily as if she were about to have a panic attack. "I have to find him," she said. "I have to tell him."

"Is that really more important than finding out who

you really are? Don't you want to know why you have been living as a half human from the Primme family and cousin of the Berzam family when you are in fact neither?"

It was true; she did want to find out. But the truth scared her. She thought about all those months when she woke up screaming in bed. It had been Edwin who wrapped his arms around her. It had been Edwin who comforted her. And it had been Edwin that got her through those times. She needed him to get through this. And yes, a part of her, a big part of her, wanted to share a guilt-free kiss with him. What would it be like to be able to kiss him without having that nagging fear of a charge of incest hanging over them?

But now she was forced to wait. She knew it would already be too late to reach him. The order that he decided to join forbade all contact with the outside world for three months. He wouldn't even have access to handwritten letters, let alone a TelEx for the next three months. She had absolutely no way of contacting him.

"I ran your DNA through a database for missing and abducted life forms and I found you," Jason said.

"What? You already know who I am?"

Jason sighed. "Well, yes, but no."

"I don't understand," Femili said.

"I think you need to sit down again for this."

Femili obeyed and took a seat on the medical table she was just lying on.

"According to this database, your name is Dahlonega Greer. You were born in the Haran archipelago right here on AiJalon."

"Okay. So I am from AiJalon. That explains why I look full-blooded AiJalonian. I don't understand what is so shocking about this piece of information."

Jason sighed again. He turned to look at his monitor as if verifying the information. Femili tried to read along with him, but it was written in a language she didn't understand which was odd because given that it was about an AiJalonian missing person, it should have been written in AiJish. It was almost as if he didn't want her to be able to read what was written.

"I don't understand. Why do you keep sighing? Why do you look so worried?"

Jason took a deep breath and said, "Because according to this information, you apparently disappeared two years before you were born."

Chapter 27

"Is that some kind of human humor?" Femili asked, trying to remain calm. "My father— well, the man I thought was my father, often uses that humor. Is this your attempt?"

Jason shook his head. "Believe it or not, I am completely serious."

"How exactly is that possible? How did I disappear two years before I was born?"

"If I knew, I would tell you, but honestly, I have no idea."

"Could it be a mistake?"

"That's what I thought at first as well. So I checked and I rechecked. I checked the information several times, in multiple languages and on different planets."

"If I went missing, someone had to report me missing, right?"

"Those files are sealed unfortunately. We would have to inquire directly with the Ministry of Justice if we want more information on your case."

"Why are we not doing that?"

"Because what if you are in danger?"

Femili hadn't thought of that possibility. If the records were faked, someone had gone through a lot of trouble to fabricate them. If they went through that much trouble there had to be a good reason, a life and death reason. If the records weren't faked, and she had actually disappeared two years before she was born, then things got even more complicated. She was some sort of anomaly. Or maybe she didn't exist at all. Jason was right. They needed more information before they got the authorities involved.

"Then what do we do?" she asked.

"I know the woman ... " Jason paused. He seemed unable to say what he really wanted to say. Femili wondered if it would be easier for him to say it in human English. "I have an acquaintance on this planet that may be able to give us some guidance. I have already contacted him."

"Maybe I should head to Minnith to talk to my parents about this," Femili said.

Jason looked at her skeptically. "You just want to go to Minnith because Edwin is there."

Somehow, now knowing that she was full AiJalonian made even the attempt at lying more difficult. "I just want him to know what we have found out."

"You love him, don't you?"

Femili felt her stomach turning as she attempted to come up with a believable response. "He is my cousin ... Or I thought he was my cousin for these past three years. Of course I love him."

"You AiJalonians are downright hilarious with your physical reactions to lying. Look, you get no judgment from me. I've read that back on Earth, people married their first cousins for centuries."

"Really? Gross."

"I know, right? Anyway, we have already established that trying to find Edwin is pointless right now. He is out of commission for three months. You will just have to wait. Talking to your parents is actually a good idea, but you can do that by TelEx."

"My parents cannot afford one with the requisite range to receive a message from this planet."

"I'll work on some ways to boost our signal. Until then, let's see what Font Darkeny has to say on the matter.

He seemed to know the history of your situation."

The waiting was torturous. Femili didn't know what to do. She couldn't find out the truth from her parents; she couldn't draw comfort from her Edwin. Her Edwin. She could say that now. They could actually love each other. But would it be too late? He had chosen the strictest order of the priesthood, one that didn't allow marriage. Would he abandon his religion for her?

Unfortunately, she would have to wait and see. Back to her thoughts about her current situation, she thought about asking the Berzams. But at this point, she didn't trust them. If they knew she wasn't at all human, would they have tried to turn her into a servant like they did? Either way they chose to answer that question, it wouldn't paint them in a good light. For either they made her a servant because she was human or they made her a servant knowing full well that she wasn't human.

There was never any reason for Femili to clean and cook for the family when a robot could do it more efficiently. Femili just accepted her plight because she thought it was the only way. And after a while, she hadn't actually minded it at all because it allowed her to be close to Edwin. She had always been able to use cleaning as an excuse to go to his room.

To distract her from the thoughts of her origin, she went to check on Thom. Just like every other day, Mac was sitting by his side. She rarely left him even to eat. Femili was beginning to wonder if Lumercans had different requirements for bodily processes which allowed her to not have to relieve herself.

"You really care about him, don't you?" Femili asked.

"I love him," Mac said, not taking her eyes off of him. "I always thought he was handsome, and kind, and strong. But I remember the precise moment I fell for him completely." She looked over at Femili. "I don't know how much you know about what we do, but we save lives. We rescue girls headed for a life of slavery."

Turning her attention back to Thom, she continued. "It was about three years ago, one of our earliest missions; we were still learning how things worked and we got into some trouble on Capernica." She leaned closer to him before saying, "Thom traded his Raven Class Guster for the lives of three girls. That's when I knew he was the one."

Femili thought back to three years ago. She remembered a time when Thom came home injured, claiming that he had crashed Edwin's guster.

"But I wasted so much time," Mac continued. "And I don't even know why. What was the point? Was I waiting for him to make the first move?" She wiped a tear away. "What a stupid, typical girl I was. I pride myself on being tough, and strong, and fearless, but when it came to Thom, I was an efyrting wistleflop."

Despite the situation, Femili couldn't help but smile at the use the Minnith profanity along with the Lumercan noun for someone who was afraid of everything.

"We could have been happy and together all this time. Instead, I waited and I caused this accident. Everything was my fault and if he dies, I don't think I will ever be able to forgive myself. But if he wakes up and he forgives me, I will never let him out of my sight for the rest of our lives."

"Forgive you for what?" Thom's voice was so weak it was barely a whisper.

"Thom!" Mac screamed. "You're awake! Femili, go get my brother."

Brother? Femili thought. Was she talking about Jason? She had no idea they were even related.

"What am I supposed to forgive you for?" Thom asked.

"I distracted you," Mac said. "If I hadn't waited until that specific moment to tell you how I felt then you would have sensed the danger and you wouldn't have gotten hurt."

"Mackelia de Tabor Wesli Clintok, that is the most ridiculous thing I have ever heard."

"What?"

"As I recall, I am the one who told you how I felt. You still haven't told me—"

"I love you," she said, interrupting him. "I've loved you for a very long time and I am sorry I didn't say it earlier, but if you forgive me, I will tell you every day for forever."

"There is nothing to forgive."

Femili left the room as things started to turn into a private, intimate moment for the two of them. Seeing them together made her even more determined to be with her Edwin.

Chapter 28

Two days later, Thom was nearly back to normal. His limbs had arrived from Lumerca and Jason had spent several hours reattaching them. He still couldn't walk properly, but he was able to at least stand and sit himself into a levitating chair so that he could get around. Mac, as promised, never left his side. Femili got the feeling that she was being extremely literal when she said she never would again.

"Let me get that for you," Mac said as she reached for his glass at breakfast. Thom's left arm and right hand had just been reattached and he still didn't have complete control over them.

"Thank you," he said before she helped him take a sip.

"And who are you?" Comtesa Berzam asked

innocently. In her defense, it was the first time she had actually made it to breakfast in months.

"This is my betrothed," Thom said without hesitation. "She is the woman I plan on spending the rest of my life with."

"And she's been here for a week, Mother," Ju'Lya added, dripping with bitterness. Things had decidedly not turned out her way. Her married sister had run off with the man she had desired and so now, her stomach turned at the sight of anyone else remotely happy in love.

"Ah, I see. You are very ... shiny," Comtesa Bertram said. All Lumercans had a certain glow about them. Many in the galaxy thought Lumercans were the most beautiful species, but Comtesa Berzam had never been a fan of their type of supposed, luminous beauty. "And what is your name, dear?" Comtesa Berzam asked.

"Mackelia de Tabor Wesli Clintok," she answered.

"Ah, de Tabor, I see." Even if Comtesa Berzam was not partial to Lumercan beauty, she was not a fool unaware of the amount of wealth from the Tabor clan. "Welcome to our home," she said with the amount of warmth especially reserved for highly suitable future daughters-in-law.

"Again, she's been here for a week." Ju'Lya finished her last bite of food, pushed her plate away and then stormed out of the dining room.

"What was that about?" Comtesa Bertram asked. Before anyone could answer Jason came running in.

"We have company," he said. Apparently, that had special meaning for Mac and Thom because they immediately went into what seemed like attack mode and followed Jason toward the front of Mansfield Park. Femili followed after them.

"And who was that human?" Comtesa Berzam asked once everyone was already out of the room. Since there was no one to answer the question, a service droid said, "Jason Barvery, youngest human graduate of the Intergalactic Medical Academy."

Pulling up to the door was a Galvin class guster, an older version of the guster Edwin used to have.

"You called the Darkenys?" Thom asked. "Why?"

"Font has information on Femili's past," Jason answered.

"Me?" Femili asked.

"Font! Long time, man," Jason said when a tall AiJalonian man exited the guster.

"Good to see you," he answered.

"You didn't have to come all the way here," Jason

said. "You could have just sent a TelEx with the info you know."

Font shook his head. "I don't think you completely understand the situation. There is no way a TelEx would suffice."

Just then a striking AiJalonian woman exited the guster. She opened her mouth to say something, then instantly froze as soon as she laid eyes on Femili. Then, in a fraction of a second, she whipped out an equalizer that had been hidden in her long coat and pointed it directly at Femili. "What are you?" she asked.

"Me? What?" was Femili's panicked response.

"Whoa, calm down here," Jason said, stepping in front of the equalizer.

"Femili, go inside," Thom said as he too moved to block her from the armed AiJalonian. Mac pulled out an equalizer as well and pointed it right back at the AiJalonian in defense of Femili.

"Everyone, calm down," the man known as Font said. "Val, you know there has to be a logical explanation for this, right?"

"What is that thing?" the woman asked. "I can't go through this again."

"Val, relax," Font put his hand on Val's and tried to

lower her equalizer but she held it firmly in place and directed squarely at Femili.

She shook her head. "Something is wrong. How can that be Dahlonega? She looks exactly the same. How could she not have aged in twenty years? This isn't right. This is not my sister."

"Sister?" Femili said. She was too paralyzed with fear to have obeyed the multiple orders for her to retreat into Mansfield Park.

"Val, we can figure this out, but you have to put down the equalizer," Font said.

She didn't move. "Madrick, a little help please?"

A person who seemed to be a mistura exited the guster. He put his arm around Val, whispered something in her ear and she instantly collapsed in tears. He took the equalizer from her and handed it to Font. "Give us a few minutes," he said, taking her back into the spacecraft.

"What was that?" Thom yelled once Val was back in the guster. "Why was that crazy lady trying to shoot my little cousin?"

"She is not crazy, just a little distraught," Font said.

"And Femili may not be your cousin," Jason said. "Well, genetically, she definitely isn't your cousin."

"What?" Thom asked. "Why didn't you tell me?"

"Mac, you can drop your weapon now," Jason said to his sister. No one noticed until then that she was still in a defensive position and pointing her equalizer at a now nonexistent threat. Mac surveyed the area for a moment and then reluctantly put it away. "Look," Jason said to Thom, "I remembered your questions about Femili and I agreed with your estimation so I did a quick DNA test. Turns out you were right. Femili is not half human and she is not your cousin. She is a full-bloodied AiJalonian by the name of Dahlonega Greer."

"Who happens to be the sister of the woman you all just met, Valdosta Greer," Font said.

"Charming woman," Mac said, still angry that someone dared draw a weapon so close to her Thom.

"Well, you would be a little on edge as well if your older sister who disappeared twenty years ago suddenly showed up and was now twelve years younger than you."

Mac and Thom were visibly confused. "Jason, do you still have me on any drugs? I don't understand what is happening."

"It's not just you, Thom," Mac said. "I am confused as well."

"Why didn't you tell me any of this?" Thom asked.

"Because you were almost dead," Jason answered. "I thought it could wait until at least your legs were sewed back on. Excuse me for prioritizing the health of my patient!"

"Fair enough but ... someone catch Femmy. She's going to faint," Thom said.

***

"I am not armed. I swear," Femili heard someone saying from outside her bedroom door. How did she get in bed? The last thing she remembered was an equalizer pointing at her. Right. Someone that was supposed to be her sister had tried to kill her. Now was she trying to enter her bedroom?

"I'll go with her," a voice she didn't recognize said.

"No, I will," a voice she recognized as her cousin Thom said.

"The hell you will. You are still recovering," Mac said.

Femili was starting to get a headache from all the bickering going on outside her door.

"Just let her in," she yelled. All the voices stopped. Seconds later, Val entered the room. "Hi," she said. "I'm Valdosta Greer."

Femili nodded. "I know. And I am supposedly your sister Dahlonega."

There was an awkward pause as both of them tried to figure out what should be said next.

"Do you know me? Have you seen me before?"

Femili didn't answer at first.

"I am not your sister," Femili said finally. "I grew up on Minnith to human and AiJalonian parents. I have nine younger brothers and sisters whose diapers I changed, who I dressed and taught to read until I was fifteen. And then I came here."

"I see."

"But the truth is ... I have seen you before."

Val's eyes enlarged in shock. "Where? How?"

Femili sighed. "When I came to this planet, I started having dreams. The dreams are more like memories that belong to someone else. And in those memories, I've seen your face and heard someone call you Valley."

Val burst into tears. "That's what my sister used to call me."

Instinctively, Femili went to comfort her. "I'm not your sister, but I know I am somehow connected to her."

"I'm sorry. I shouldn't be crying," Val said, wiping away tears. "I should be happy that a part of my sister lives on. I just thought I had confirmed her death seven years ago. I thought I was through with the grieving process. And then

I saw you and ... and you look exactly like she did on the day she disappeared."

"It's okay. I understand."

"How is this possible?" Val asked.

Chapter 29

"Madrick, this is my little sister Mac," Jason said, wrapping an arm around Madrick's shoulder. "Mac, I saved his life like seven years ago on Oroton 4. He was my first double lung transplant after graduating the IMA as the youngest graduate in its history."

"Nine hundred and eighty-eight!" Thom yelled. "He's said that nine hundred and eighty-eight times since I met him."

"Dear Gaion, does he still mention the IMA in every other breath?" Font asked.

"Yes, he does usually right after calling me his little sister which is not at all accurate since I'm actually his aunt."

"Look, guys," Jason said, sensing the growing

animosity in the room. "I don't have much. Each and every one of you is either rich, or married, or rich and married. All I have is my IMA accomplishment," he said, reaching into his coat pocket and pulling out his medal.

"Do you really carry that around?" Font asked.

Mac nodded emphatically. "He does. He really does."

Jason sneered at her then started the speech he had prepared. "Every hundred years or so, there is some scientific leap forward in cloning. Then something catastrophic always happens like the clone wars of Centauri or the deformities on Revua. Then when something like that happens cloning is outlawed galaxy wide until someone tries it again."

"What are you getting at, Jason?" Thom asked.

"Twenty years ago, a slaver named Leaven CoZark from the planet Kemek thought it would be more profitable and efficient to clone his slaves before selling them."

"I think I know where you're going with this," Font said. "He cloned Dahlonega, didn't he?"

Jason nodded. "I am still not sure what method he used for his process or what planet it was done on or what scientist was behind—"

"Well, what *do* you know then?" Mac asked impatiently.

Jason glared at his little sister. "Whatever method it was, the clone was born as a baby instead of grown in a lab. So, Femili may be a genetic clone of Dahlonega, but she is more like her daughter than Dahlonega herself."

Thom, Mac, Font, and Madrick sat in silence for a moment as they each individually tried to process what they had just heard. Jason waited patiently for the numerous questions that he knew would be coming, but they didn't. There were no questions at all, which was very ... weird.

"So ... " Madrick said before pausing, obviously unable to put into words what he truly wanted and needed to know just like everyone else in the room apparently. It was almost as if everyone was too confused to even know what to ask.

Finally, Thom snapped his fingers with his new right hand as an idea popped into his head. "How did she end up on Minnith? Why did she grow up thinking she was the daughter of my uncle and aunt?"

"Yes, good question," Jason said. "I am slightly prepared for that one. I researched the birth records of Minnith. They have a pretty antiquated system, but I still found some things. Femili wasn't born on Minnith to your aunt and uncle. There is no record of her birth on that planet at all. In fact, looking at the ship manifests from eighteen years ago, I found that your Aunt and Uncle Primme boarded a vessel set out for Minnith alone and then disembarked ten hours later with a child. So, unless your aunt gave birth on board, which we know she didn't since Femili is not genetically related to her, someone gave them a baby on the way to Minnith. For any details beyond that, we would have to ask your aunt and uncle."

"So ..." Madrick said again. "Did Dahlonega give birth to herself?"

Jason took a deep breath. "It seems strange, but essentially, yes. Yes, she did."

"Shouldn't there be some sort of, I don't know, side effects from that?"

"Good question. Yes, theoretically, there could be any number of side effects. But it seems with Femili, the only side effects presented were neurological and they did not manifest until she came to AiJalon."

"What do you mean neurological?" Font asked.

"Thom, remember how you always wondered how Femili knew so much about the galaxy when she was born and raised on a planet of priests? This is why. She essentially had all the knowledge of Dahlonega in her mind and somehow, maybe through AiJalon's magnetic core, when she came to this planet, it was unlocked."

"It also explains the night terrors," Thom said. "She used to describe them as watching someone else's memories. They were Dahlonega's memories."

"Poor Fem," Mac said. "She must have been so tormented for three years on this planet. Not knowing why someone else's memories were floating through her mind."

"I have something to say," Font said out of the blue. Everyone just looked at him, waiting for him to say it but he didn't.

"Well, say it," Jason said finally.

Font took a deep breath. "I don't really know how."

"That's not like you," Madrick said. "What is it about?"

"Femili is not the only clone of Dahlonega."

"What do you mean?" Madrick asked. "How do you know?"

Font sighed. "Remember when we were on Necropolis?"

Madrick nodded. "After you left the room with Val, the maintenance droid said there was another DNA match."

"Why didn't you say anything?"

"I was hoping it was just a clerical error. I didn't want to put Val through any more heartache after what could just be a mistake."

"A mistake? On Necropolis?" Jason said. "Not possible. Those dudes on that planet are meticulous. There is a whole course in the IMA on Necropolis classification methods. I got an A in it."

Mac rolled her eyes. "No one cares, Jason. No one. In fact, I don't even care that there are other clones at this point. We will worry about that later. Right now, the clone that is important is Femili. What is she going to do?"

"Since she is biologically my sister-in-law ... and my niece-in-law, I guess, I know she is welcome to live with us if the Berzams want her to leave Mansfield Park since she is not technically family."

Jason smiled. "I have a feeling she will be part of the Berzam family soon enough."

"What? What are you talking about?" Thom asked.

"You don't know?" Jason asked.

"Know what?"

Mac giggled. "My poor darling is pretty oblivious when it comes to matters of love."

"Love? Who is in love?" Thom was getting frustrated.

"How is he so observant of the most minor details but completely clueless about emotions?" Jason teased.

"What are you guys talking about? Come on. Tell

me."

Mac sighed. "Edwin and Femili are in love," she said. "I found that to be quite obvious from the moment I stepped foot into Mansfield Park. I have no idea how you didn't see it when you lived among them for three years."

"Yeah, me too," Jason added.

"I also knew," Madrick added. "It's part of the reason Val and Femili left for Minnith this morning on the Calibri. She wants to find him and tell him they are not related."

"The Calibri? What is the Calibri?" Thom asked.

Font gave an annoyed sigh as Madrick smiled brightly and said, "It's the name of Font's guster. I named it myself."

"I never agreed to that name," Font said.

"Doesn't matter. It's perfect. Get it, everyone?" Madrick said looking around at everyone in the room. "Calibri is an ancient type of font and his name is Font in human English."

"That's clever. I like it," Jason said. "Sis, we should name your ship Cheese. You can be Mac and Cheese."

"Never," Mac responded flatly.

"What is Mac and Cheese?" Font asked.

"I'll make you some later, Bro," Madrick answered.

"Can we get back to the matter at hand?" Thom said. "Am I really the last to know that Edwin sees Femili as more than a cousin?"

"Yes," everyone said in unison.

Chapter 30

Femili loved her parents. They had taken good care of her and treated her like she was their own. So, of course, she never had any reason to think otherwise. But the truth was, she wasn't their child. And they had lied to her for her entire life. Hoping on the spirit of Gaion that there was a good reason for their deception, she set out with Val, her new sister/aunt to Minnith to talk to them face-to-face. Of course, she had ulterior motives for going to Minnith.

Edwin was there.

He was in an abbey taking his priestly orders. If all of this had been revealed just a few hours earlier, she could have stopped him.

Now, he had started his sequester in a religion that

didn't allow him contact with the outside world for three months. Knowing what she now knew, Femili didn't know if she could stay away from him for that long.

"Are you still thinking about Edwin?" Val asked moments before they had arrived on Minnith. Femili nodded. "Don't worry. I can get you to him. I am rather good at breaking and entering. And besides, how good can the security at an abbey be anyway?" Val said. "First, let's talk to your parents and get the full story."

"Femili, dear. You are back so soon?" her mother asked as soon as she entered the house. "How is your cousin? Has he recovered?"

Femili took a deep breath. "We both know he is not my cousin."

The change in her mother's demeanor indicated she knew the conversation they were about to have was going to be difficult. "Go outside and play with your sister," her mother told her two youngest siblings. As the children exited, Val entered. Ge'ordana Primme stared at her as if she knew exactly who had walked into the door. "You must be her sister."

"Excuse me?" Val asked. "Do you know who I am?"

"I don't know you, per se, but she spoke of you. She

wanted to protect you."

Tears welled in Val's eyes again. "Please tell us everything."

As Val and her mother sat down at the dining table which was also the living room table and at night the bed for two of her siblings, Femili made tea and brought it out for the three of them.

"It was eighteen years ago," Ge'ordana began. "I had just eloped with your father. I knew I would be rejected by the family and ostracized. So I didn't even tell anyone. We just ran away. We didn't know where we were going. We actually boarded three different ships before we got on the one to Minnith. We thought it would be the best place for my human husband to make a living. Actually, now that I look back, it was probably Gaion's direction because it brought us to you." She reached out and touched Femili's hand before continuing.

"There was a young AiJalonian on board holding a brand-new baby. She was scared and alone. Probably, because I, too, was AiJalonian, she confided in me. She told me that you were a special creation. That people were trying to find her and kill her but that you had to be protected at all costs. She said that no one knew you existed so you could be safe as long as you weren't found with her. She said she couldn't return to AiJalon because if she went home, her younger sister would be in danger as well. I suppose that was you," Ge'ordana said, looking at Val.

"She told me so many things that I honestly thought she was mentally ill and suffering from pregnancy sickness, but I couldn't turn her away. I listened to her story as I held you in my arms. Then, right before my eyes, the collar around her neck lit up and her body went limp. I was so panicked that I held you tighter and pretended you were mine when two large Harvothites came and dragged her away. I didn't know what else to do."

"Do you remember anything else?" Femili asked. "Do you remember what happened to her after they dragged her away?"

Ge'ordana Primme nodded. "I am not sure what happened immediately after they dragged her away. But I do know that she didn't survive the journey. The vessel stopped on a burial planet and her corpse was one that was unloaded. I made sure. If there was any hope that your mother was still alive, I wanted to know so that I could reunite you one day. But there was no hope. I saw her body shot out into space toward the burial planet, Necropolis. I searched the ship's manifest to find her name, but there was no record of a teenage AiJalonian that fit her description. There was no record of anyone giving birth. There was no way for me to try to find your father."

"I didn't have a father," Femili said.

"What are you talking about? Of course, you had a father at some point."

Femili shook her head. "I'm a clone."

She was a clone. It was the first time she had said it out loud. She still wasn't sure if she had accepted it, but at least she could say the words. It didn't make her any less of a living being. On some planets they were called alternative living beings. But they were still living beings. And there were many types of clones. Some had no personalities and were only made for parts. Some were basically like living robots. Femili did as much research as she could on the way to Minnith. She was a completely new type of clone. Biologically, she was exactly the same as Dahlonega, but mentally, psychologically, and emotionally she was a completely different person. That was all that really mattered, right? She didn't have to think of herself as some sort of science experiment. She could grow to love herself for the new type of being that she was. Honestly, she wasn't convinced. She had to force herself to not think of herself as a freak. The only thing that helped her keep her sanity was the prospect of kissing her Edwin without the subsequent guilt. How amazing would that feel? But then, what if Edwin didn't feel the same way? What if he wanted nothing to do with a clone?

Val made good on her promise. Breaking into a monastery was indeed easier than expected. Of course, there would probably be a special place in hell reserved for them for doing such a thing, but Femili could deal with that later. Right now, she needed Edwin.

Somehow, even from AiJalon, Val's husband Madrick was able to hack into the antiquated computer system of the Orthodox Abbey where Edwin was residing. He was able to give Femili exact directions to his room. It was during evening prayer time so all of the priests in training were in their rooms.

Femili silently entered his room as Edwin kneeled in prayer toward the moon. When finished, he stood, turned around and saw her standing there. Femili held her finger to her lips indicating he should be quiet in case he had the urge to scream, thus alerting the entire abbey to her presence. But Edwin didn't even seem surprised to see her which thoroughly confused her. He smiled slightly then began adjusting his long, brown robe.

"Aren't you the least bit surprised to see me?" she asked.

He shook his head. "I just finished praying to Gaion. I asked that if it wasn't a sin to love you, that he please give me a sign. I asked him to give me just a glimpse of you. I didn't expect my prayers to be answered so soon. And I didn't expect the vision to be so real."

Femili shook her head. "I'm not a vision, you dope. I'm really here."

"Not possible. You're on AiJalon. Even if you were on Minnith, how would you possibly get into the abbey? No one is allowed in here for three months."

"I broke in."

He chuckled. "Now I know you are just a figment of my imagination. Though I had no idea my imagination was so vivid." He sat down on his bed which took up more than half of the miniscule room and began reading a holy book, completely ignoring her.

"Edwin, I'm serious. I'm really on Minnith and I really broke into this abbey with the help of Val."

"And who is Val?"

"She's my sister ... or ... well, she's my aunt depending on how you look at it."

Instead of responding, he went back to reading.

"Okay, how do I explain this so that it makes sense?" Femili thought for a moment. "I can't, so here it goes. I am not your cousin. I am a clone of a woman named Dahlonega Greer who is the sister of Valdosta Greer. I am a genetic bio clone which means that Dahlonega's own DNA was replicated ... Look: the how and the why is not important right now. What is important is that I am *not* your cousin."

He still didn't turn his attention away from his book. "Edwin, did you hear me? I am not your cousin. We are not related. Do you know what this means? Answer me."

"The only thing worse than hallucinating that the woman you love is in your room is talking back to that hallucination. Which I will no longer be doing," he said without looking at Femili.

Femili let out a string of Minnithite profanities that she didn't even know she knew before snatching the holy book out of his hands and straddling him on the bed. "Can a hallucination do this?" she asked before firmly planting her lips on his.

He pushed her away and then screamed while jumping up on top of the bed as if he were running away from a mouse. She covered her lips with her finger again, indicating he should be quiet.

"Femili?" he said as if waking up from a dream "You're really here?

"Brother Edwin, are you okay in there?" someone called from the hallway.

"Get rid of him," Femili whispered.

"Yes, yes, I'm fine, Pastor Paul," he called. "I just saw a small ... rodent. I'm fine now."

"All Gaion's creatures. All Gaion's creatures," Pastor Paul said as he walked away.

Once the footsteps receded Edwin said, "What are you doing here?"

Femili sighed. "Have you not been listening to a word I've said?"

"No. Not really. I thought you were not real."

"Well, I am real and I'm really *not* your cousin," she said.

"We're not related?"

"Edwin, that's what I—"

Instead of letting her finish, he swept her up into his arms and kissed her even more passionately than she had just seconds before.

"Edwin, wait," she said, pushing him away momentarily. "You need to hear the whole story. I'm a clone. Can you still accept me?"

"I don't care what you are, as long as you're mine." He pulled her in for another kiss. "I love you," he said when he had kissed her to satisfaction.

"I love you too."

"I'm so relieved to be able to say that without feeling like I'm going to hell."

"Well, we are making out in an abbey just days before you take a vow of celibacy so there might be a couple of spots opening up for us again."

"You're right. We should get out of here." Edwin flung open his bedroom door and dragged her out into the hallway. "I have an announcement," he called. "I'm getting married!" It was a rather odd thing to yell out in an abbey for soon-to-be Orthodox Minnithite priests for which marriage was prohibited, but he yelled it out gleefully all the same. Slowly, his soon-to-be priest brothers poked their heads out of their rooms. Some looked confused, others looked angry, and a few looked happy. Edwin approached one of the happy faces and said, "Will you marry us?"

"Right now?" Femili asked.

"Femili, I swear to Gaion I can't stay away from you for a second longer. Either marry me right now or tonight we will be cementing our path to hell. The choice is yours."

"Well, if you put it that way, let's get married."

Chapter 31

Mr. Rushworth was granted a speedy divorce with full propriety given the flagrant infidelity and Marziah's admittance to it. On his way to the Ministry of Records to file the paperwork, he was met with the one-woman protest of Kibby La'rue, a marine biologist from the planet Revua. The focus of her protest? The misclassification of a breed of flickerfish and her desire—nay, insistence that it be properly classified immediately lest generations of marine biology students go on misinformed. After Mr. Rushworth filed his paperwork, he decided to join what he deemed to be a just and warranted protest. Three months later, he also joined her in matrimony.

Ju'Lya, though at one point almost completely

inseparable from her sister in personality and disposition, soon became quite independent and different from her. After seeing how diligent, brilliant, and hardworking he was, she fancied herself in love with Jason Barvery. While he was still caring for her brother during his recovery, she followed him around every day like a lovesick puppy. Jason had zero interest in courting a rather young and spoiled AiJalonian daughter of a noble so he tried to let her down easy. Though she didn't pick up on his lack of interest quite as fast as he had hoped. The one-sided attraction to a guy like Jason Barvery was enough to improve Ju'Lya's character into a pretty decent person. Her intellect improved, her compassion increased, and her daily conversation revolved around things other than the income or availability of local gentlemen. Soon, instead of wanting to quickly rush off into marriage, she decided to study and try to get accepted into the medical academy.

The ill-fated relationship of Hin'Rik Crawly and Mrs. Rushworth lasted about as long as most people expected: about a month.

In that time, Marziah Rushworth grew to hate Hin'Rik Crawly with about as much passion as she formerly desired him. Though Femili was nowhere near them and quite out of the picture, Marziah still felt Femili was the cause of their demise given how much and how often Hin'Rik mentioned her and compared her to Marziah. The final straw was when Hin'Rik called out 'Femili!' during a moment of passion. It wasn't even the first time that it had happened, but it was the first time that Hin'Rik not only refused to apologize for it but actually suggested that it was for the best if Marziah just let him pretend. Her pride would not allow her to live in another woman's shadow.

She immediately reached out to her father to ask for forgiveness and permission to return to Mansfield Park. She had no reason to believe this request would be denied given that her father had never denied her anything before in the past. But things had apparently changed and Femili Primme's influence had not only gained control of her lover's mind but also her father's.

Marziah was apparently not being allowed to return to Mansfield Park for fear that her presence and behavior would negatively influence her younger sister and perhaps upset Femili Primme. Femili Primme again! Although, now she was no longer Femili Primme but Femili Berzam! Had her father adopted her as a replacement daughter? What on AiJalon was going on?

"You can't just abandon your own flesh and blood,"

Mrs. Norris was saying to Comte Berzam as he was trying his best to ignore her. "Yes, she has made mistakes. Yes, she has brought a measure of shame upon the family. But she is still your child. If you abandon her, what is she to do? She may become even more desperate and bring greater reproach on the Berzam name. I beg you to at least give her a place to live."

"I am not abandoning her," Comte Berzam said, still not looking at Mrs. Norris. He had actually had his fill of her and could barely tolerate her any further. At one point in their lives, he had thought she was exceedingly wise and valued her opinion. He had even trusted her to practically raise his daughters much to their obvious detriment.

But ever since Femili had moved in with them over three years ago, his estimation of Mrs. Norris had steadily decreased. He did not appreciate her apparent double dealing. "I have actually secured an apartment for her on Tentor."

"Tentor?" Mrs. Norris almost recoiled in horror. "There are so many humans on Tentor it is practically a New Earth. How will she ever survive? And it is so far away. Won't she be lonely? And an apartment. How will she know how to deal with such a small, incommodious residence? This simply will not do."

"I completely agree with you," Comte Berzam said, looking at her for the first time. "She will need a teacher, a guide. Someone who is used to dealing with the trials of a small income and living in a small residence. Since you have been enduring such a plight for these fifteen plus years, I feel you are the most qualified tutor."

"Me? What?"

"I have already booked your ship. You leave in an hour. I suggest you pack." With that he stood and exited the parlor.

Not even Femili had tears for Aunt Norris, not even when she was gone forever which, for all intents and purposes, was the same as being banished to Tentor.

With Mrs. Norris out of the abbey on Mansfield Park, it became the residence of the new Mr. and Mrs. Edwin Berzam. Still in newlywed bliss, they hadn't completely decided what they would do with their lives so having a residence available was a great help. As each day passed and they learned more and more about the work that Thom, Val, Mac and Jason did, they both were independently thinking they wanted to do something similar except for clones. In getting their marriage legally recognized on AiJalon, they both realized how difficult it was for a clone to simply ...

exist. They had no independent identity separate from the original living being. The only reason Femili was allowed interplanetary travel was because she was registered as the child of the Primmes. Other clones did not have that advantage. There were forced to live more as property than as a living being. Femili wanted to change that and give clones the opportunity to have their own independent existence.

Eventually, they would bring it up, be in total agreement as they often were and soon join the fight, but until that time, they just enjoyed the guilt-free love that had eluded them for three long years.

It was during this time of marital bliss that there was one day a knock on the door. Much to the surprise of both of them, it was Hin'Rik Crawly.

"Hello," was all he said to the both of them while standing outside their door. It had been months since they'd seen each other and so much had changed. But not his confidence, style, and general good looks. He was still charming enough to charm the pants off of most people. But not Femili Primme and that was possibly why he was at her door.

"What are you doing here?" Edwin asked. Between Edwin and Femili, Edwin probably had the most reasons to hate Hin'Rik Crawly. For he had defiled Edwin's sister, ruining her for all AiJalonian society, and he had toyed with the emotions of his Femmy.

"That is an excellent question," Hin'Rik answered. "I am actually here for her."

"You mean my wife?"

"You probably haven't heard," Femili began, "but a lot has changed in these—"

"Yes, I know," he interrupted impatiently. "You are not his cousin. You are a clone and you are married to each other. I have done my due diligence. I know the story."

"Well, then, what on AiJalon could possibly bring you to our doorstep?" Femili asked.

"I love you," Hin'Rik said by way of response. "Once I started loving you, I couldn't stop and I don't plan on stopping."

"Just what exactly are you saying?" Edwin had never been a violent person. Until about three months ago, he was sure he would spend his life as a pacifist, celibate priest for Gaion's sake. But listening to another man proclaim love for his wife was too much to bear. He wanted to rip Hin'Rik Crawly's tongue out of his mouth.

"Loving you was the only time in my life when I felt good about myself," Hin'Rik said, ignoring Edwin's interruption while his gaze locked on Femili.

"Well, that is irrelevant now because she is *married*."

"Do you think that has ever stopped me before?"

Edwin lunged for Hin'Rik and Femili held him back. "He's not worth it," she said as she pulled him into the abbey and closed the door.

"This isn't over!" they heard Hin'Rik yell from outside. "You will love me back one day, Femili Primme!"

But it was over. For nothing could ever separate Edwin and Femili Primme Berzam for as long as they both lived.

Epilogue

He really wasn't quite sure how it happened, but one day Jason looked around and realized he missed Ju'Lya. Every day for weeks she had been following him like shadow. Most days she would feign interest in her brothers care just so she could enter the lab and simply be stare at Jason himself. Other days she would ask for private lessons with the pretense of applying to a medical academy. At first, didn't believe her interest him could be genuine. How could it be? She was a spoiled, rich AiJalonian and he was an orphan human. No creature in the galaxy would be silly enough to fall for him.

After a while, Jason wished it to be true. He wanted her to care for him just as he was, but he didn't dare believe it. He had learned from his life on Lumerca that love and marriage would be impossible for someone like him. So even when missing her by his side in the lab turned into longing to see her, he didn't let it show. And when that longing to see her morphed into never wanting leave her presence, he continuously minimized his feelings and disregarded them. He was just being the typical emotional human being, he thought. *These feelings will pass.*

"Are you going to marry her?" Mac asked Jason as he checked the inventory of his make-shift lab. Nearly two months after Thom's accident, they were still living in Mansfield Park. Neither of them minded not returning to Lumerca as it was obvious the Berzam siblings meant so much to each of them.

"Marry? Me? Whom?" Jason asked not looking at his aunt.

Mac crossed her arms and glared at him. "You are too smart to play dumb."

"I really don't know what you're talking about."

Mac snatched the TelEx out of his hand and tossed it on the bed in the center of the room. "Ju'Lya. You are in love with her."

"I am not."

She smiled. "Your lies may work well on AiJalonians, but not me. I know you."

Jason didn't respond. He stood up and aimlessly walked around the lab looking for something to count, or evaluate, or fix. He wondered if it was time to do another fitness test on Thom.

"Thom has been walking and using all his limbs for three and a half weeks now," Mac said. "Yet we are still here." She followed him around the lab to make sure he could clearly hear all the evidence she was about to present. "We could have easily returned to Lumerca and continued his care remotely. Yet, we are still here."

"I thought you'd want more time with Thom."

"Nice try. Thom could easily come with us. Even if he and I stayed here, you could return to Lumerca by yourself."

He didn't have a response to this line of reasoning.

"You've also started teaching Ju'Lya English, AiJalonian and Engorian medical terms."

"So?"

Mac huffed then took a seat on the bed that once held her precious Thom when he was fighting for his life. "Whenever I've asked you to teach me or even explain a simple term or procedure, you either ignore me or say you don't have time. Yet, you spend hours a day tutoring her. Jason, dear nephew, you are not one to use your time and efforts so frivolously. You love her, you want to be near her, and you are using any excuse to do so."

No response.

"Fine, don't admit it." She hopped of the bed and headed for the door. "Just give me a heads up when you do marry her. If my nephew marries my sister-in-law, I'm going to need at least a week to figure out our family tree."

Jason flopped on the bed next to his TelEx. It frustrated him how emotional he was being. Who was he kidding? He was in love. He loved Ju'Lya Berzam. And it wasn't just because she was pretty or because she was the first woman to ever show any romantic interest in a clan-less human like himself. Even though he and Mac were related, because Jason's parents abandoned him at birth, he could never be part of a clan on Lumerca and thus never worthy of marriage. But Ju'Lya didn't care about any of that. She just wanted him. And she was the one actually working so hard to prove this.

Her efforts reminded him of himself before he entered the medical academy. No one believed he could do it. It was extremely rare for a human to even get accepted into the IMA let alone one so young. He constantly had to prove himself. He remembered so many sleepless nights spent memorizing facts or performing virtual surgeries. It was exhausting overcoming one prejudice after another. And that was exactly what Ju'Lya was going through. She was working so hard to prove herself to him and overcome the assumption that she was an emptied-headed child who couldn't possibly know what she wanted. But it was obvious that she *did* know what she wanted. Ju'Lya wanted him. She wanted Jason Barvery, a clan-less human born on the clan-oriented planet of Lumerca. It was simply amazing and…beautiful. Her love for him was almost as beautiful as she was.

Just as he was about to seek her out and reveal his true feelings, he received a message. Looking back, he wished he'd never opened that message, for it irrevocably changed the next decade of his life.

Author's Note

Thank you for taking the time to read Mansfield Park in Space. As an independent author, the most effective way to promote my book is through word of mouth. So, if you enjoyed my work, please tell a friend and consider leaving a review. Thanks!

Jane Austen In Space books

Pride and Prejudice in Space

Sense and Sensibility in Space

Mansfield Park in Space

Persuasion in Space Coming 2024

Emma in Space Coming 2025

Other Novels by Sybil Nelson.

Click to Purchase.

Priscilla the Great

Priscilla the Great: The Kiss of Life

Priscilla the Great: Too Little Too Late

Priscilla the Great: Bring the Pain

Priscilla the Great: The Time Traveling Bullet

Priscilla the Great presents Twin Shorts

Priscilla the Great versus Armpit Hair

Priscilla the Great versus the World

Dark Marco vol 1

Dark Marco vol 2

Ebonee and Ivory